CYRANO DE BERGERAC

BESTSELLING ENRICHED CLASSICS FROM POCKET BOOKS

Jane Eyre
Charlotte Brontë

Wuthering Heights
Emily Brontë

The Good Earth
Pearl Buck

The Awakening and Selected Stories of Kate Chopin
Kate Chopin

Heart of Darkness and *The Secret Sharer*
Joseph Conrad

Great Expectations
Charles Dickens

A Tale of Two Cities
Charles Dickens

The Count of Monte Cristo
Alexandre Dumas

The Scarlet Letter
Nathaniel Hawthorne

The Odyssey
Homer

The Prince
Niccolò Machiavelli

Frankenstein
Mary Shelley

The Jungle
Upton Sinclair

Uncle Tom's Cabin
Harriet Beecher Stowe

Adventures of Huckleberry Finn
Mark Twain

CYRANO DE BERGERAC

Edmond Rostand

TRANSLATED INTO ENGLISH VERSE
BY HOWARD THAYER KINGSBURY

Supplementary material written by Rebecca Johnson

Series edited by Cynthia Brantley Johnson

POCKET BOOKS
NEW YORK LONDON TORONTO SYDNEY

POCKET BOOKS, a division of Simon & Schuster, Inc.
1230 Avenue of the Americas, New York, NY 10020

Supplementary materials copyright © 2004 by Simon & Schuster, Inc.

ISBN 13: 978-0-7434-8775-7
ISBN 10:   0-7434-8775-3

First Pocket Books printing November 2004

10 9 8 7 6 5 4 3 2

POCKET and colophon are registered trademarks of Simon & Schuster, Inc.

Front cover art by Stephanie Henderson

Manufactured in the United States of America

For information regarding special discounts for bulk purchases, please contact Simon & Schuster Special Sales at 1-800-456-6798 or business@simonandschuster.com

CONTENTS

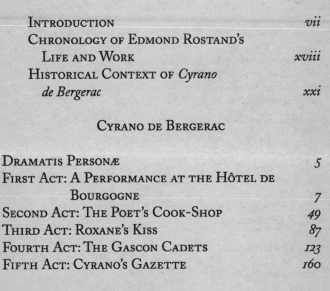

INTRODUCTION
Cyrano de Bergerac:
The Epitome of Panache

In the one hundred years since its opening night in Paris, Edmond Rostand's *Cyrano de Bergerac* (1897) has been performed more than any other theatrical work in France. It has been translated into dozens of languages several times over and has been adapted repeatedly for film and television, for the musical theater and the opera. The title character is a prized role among actors of the past century and has been played by the world's greatest leading men, from Jean Coquelin to Jean-Paul Belmondo to Gérard Depardieu.

On the surface, the enduring appeal and classic stature of *Cyrano de Bergerac* is mystifying. It takes as its hero a man who was eccentric and dramatic, but certainly not "great," a man who is best known for his oddball science fiction in which men traveled to the moon. The play does not neatly fit into any prescribed category: neither precisely tragedy nor comedy, it was described by Rostand as "heroic comedy." Rostand composed *Cyrano de Bergerac* in his native French, in verse that imitated the rhyming alexandrine couplets popular in the seventeenth century when the "real" Cyrano lived. But Rostand's poetry struck subsequent translators as so quirky and unwieldy that many have chosen to do away with verse entirely and make theirs strictly prose adaptations.

Although the play was overwhelmingly and unanimously acclaimed at its debut (the standing ovation at its first performance is said to have lasted one hour), critical reaction over the years has been mixed. Reviewers are continually frustrated by *Cyrano*'s sentimental romance and improbable scenes. Moreover, the play's historical basis is obscure. There once really was a Cyrano de Bergerac, who lived in France hundreds of years before Edmond Rostand immortalized him in his famous play of the same name. Savinien Cyrano was born in Paris in 1619, but he did live in Bergerac for a good deal of his life. A skilled swordsman, the historical Cyrano had quite a reputation for swashbuckling. He did have a prominent nose, and he did have a way with words (he published plays, poems, political pamphlets, and several seminal science fiction novels).

In the theater, this minor historical figure becomes larger-than-life, larger than his own myth, so much so that the legend of Cyrano de Bergerac as created by Edmond Rostand has largely eclipsed actual historical heroes of seventeenth-century France. Cyrano is grotesque, but he is a dashing, showy fighter. He deceives, but with such an abundance of well-versed wit, with such loyalty, and for such honorable cause that he is forgiven. In short, when all else is lost, he holds fast to that intangible but timeless French quality: Cyrano has *panache*—a word originally used to mean a large, decorative plume on a hat, but which now means a daring, witty display of style and verve. This is why, according to many of the play's admirers, the legacy of this half-historical, half-fictitious character has claimed such an enduring grip on the world's, and especially France's, imagination.

The Life and Work of Edmond Rostand

Edmond Rostand was born in Marseille in 1868, the son of a prominent economist, journalist, and poet. From an early age, Rostand began writing and publishing poetry in small magazines. He moved to Paris, where he studied with René Doumie, a well-known literary critic of the 1880s, worked briefly in a bank, and received his degree in law. Although he was admitted to the bar, Rostand never formally practiced law; by this time, he was seriously writing poetry and plays, and thanks to his family's comfortable financial health, he never had to take a job, left free to concentrate on his writing.

Rostand's first published play, *Le Gant Rouge* (1888), was a collaboration with Henry Lee, who was the half brother of Rostand's future wife, the highly regarded poet Rosemonde Gérard. Rostand's wedding gift to Rosemonde was literary: a volume of poetry, which he self-published as *Les Musardises* (*The Idlers*—1890). Neither the play or the collection received much acclaim. His next play, *Les Deux Pierrots*, a one-act farce, was initially accepted by the influential state-subsidized theater Comédie-Française, but Rostand withdrew it after some pointed out its similarity to the work of another playwright.

At last Rostand achieved public recognition with *Les*

Romanesques (1894), a three-act comedy written in verse, which was produced at the Comédie-Française and garnered Rostand a prize of five thousand francs. *Les Romanesques* satirized Romeo and Juliet, imagining that the parents of Shakespeare's star-crossed lovers pose as enemies to ensure that their children rebel and fall in love. The success of *Les Romanesques* permitted Rostand to begin to work with some of the best actors in the French theater in his next plays, *La Princesse Lointaine* (*The Princess Far Away*—1895) and *La Samaritaine* (1897), including such stars as Sarah Bernhardt, Lucien Guitry, and the preeminent comic actor Benoît Constant Coquelin, who asked Rostand to write him a play. His wish was granted, with *Cyrano de Bergerac*.

In 1896, the year Rostand began writing *Cyrano de Bergerac*, he was diagnosed with neurasthenia, a respiratory and anxiety disorder, the first of many ailments that would mark a lifetime of poor health. Also in this year, France was divided over the controversy ensuing from the infamous Dreyfus Affair. Along with writers such as Émile Zola and Marcel Proust, Rostand became a "Dreyfusard": he took the side of Alfred Dreyfus, a Jewish army officer who was falsely accused and convicted of treason, despite evidence that suggested his innocence. Rostand, like Proust and Zola (who published a famous letter in the French newspaper *L'Aurore* accusing several prominent figures of railroading Dreyfus), believed that Alfred Dreyfus was a victim of injustice caused by anti-Semitism.

At the time, literally everyone went to the theater. In the 1880s more than half a million Parisians sat in a theater audience at least once a week; and a million of them attended the theater at least monthly. Parisian theatergoers were a diverse crowd, attending literary histories, melodramas, and adventures alike. Rostand's play, notable for challenging categorization, anachronistically combined both modern and traditional elements, hearkening back to a golden age in France, without accurately recording its history. Yet no one, certainly not the playwright himself, had an inkling of the popular reception *Cyrano* would inspire.

Edmond Rostand was only twenty-nine years old when *Cyrano de Bergerac* had its debut performance on December 28, 1897. The actress scheduled to play the part of Roxane had fallen ill, and at the last minute Rostand's wife, Rosemonde, stepped in. Just before the curtain went up, Rostand is said to have apologized to Benoît Constant Coquelin for involving him in this "disastrous adventure." *Cyrano de Bergerac* received an overwhelming standing ovation; its rapturous audience did not leave the theater until the wee hours of the morning. The play would go on to run for an astounding four hundred consecutive performances. Rostand became an overnight success, hailed as a successor to Victor Hugo and decorated as a knight of the French Legion of Honor.

In his later plays, Rostand was unable to match the bravado of Cyrano. His work was slowed by his increasingly ailing health. After 1900's modestly successful *L'Aiglon*, produced with Sarah Bernhardt in the lead role, Rostand retired to Cambo-les-Bains in the Pyrenees mountains for several years of recuperation. He left the Pyrenees for his acceptance, at age thirty-three, into the Académie Française, but returned to labor over his next play, *Chantecler*, which he wrote for Jean Coquelin. Coquelin died before *Chantecler*'s first performance, and this was the first of many setbacks in Rostand's later life. After *Chantecler,* Rostand wrote only two more plays, 1910's *Le Bois Sacré* and *La Dernière Nuit de Don Juan,* which was not produced until after his death.

Due to his poor health, Rostand was not admitted into the French army during World War I. He became rather fixated on the war, however, and wrote a collection of patriotic poems *(Le Vol de la Marseillaise),* and at one point in 1915, he even visited the front. In 1918, just after the war's end, Edmond Rostand died of the respiratory illness that had plagued him most of his life. Surviving him were his wife, Rosemonde; his sons, Maurice, a writer and critic, and Jean, a scientist; and of course, the heroic comedy that captured France, *Cyrano de Bergerac.*

Historical and Literary Context of *Cyrano de Bergerac*

The Age of Richelieu

Cyrano de Bergerac begins in 1640, at the height of the Age of Richelieu in France, just three years before Louis XIV would be crowned. These last years prior to Louis XIV's reign can be viewed retrospectively as a turbulent "last gasp" before the age of absolute monarchy and extravagant rule was ushered in. This was the time before France's ruling elite completely abandoned religious tolerance and greatly widened the gap between the monarchy and the people, as the grand construction of Louis XIV's Versailles would symbolize.

The historical Cyrano was born in 1619 in Paris.

Three years later, in 1622, Armand-Jean du Plessis, who took the name Richelieu from his family estate, was made cardinal. By 1624 he was prime minister of France under the rule of Louis XIII. Richelieu was a ruthless leader who exerted a centralizing influence on French politics. The heart of his domestic policy aimed at destroying the political powers of the French Huguenot peoples, who as practicing Protestants enjoyed special political privileges that had been set forth under Henry IV's Edict of Nantes in 1598. Richelieu put a stop to Huguenot uprisings in 1622, 1625, and 1627. At last in 1628, Richelieu captured the Huguenot stronghold at La Rochelle. The Peace at Alais, which ended the La Rochelle uprising, effectively quashed the political powers of the Huguenots, but conceded to them continued religious tolerance.

Early in his rule, he was beset by enemies, including the king's brother, Gaston d'Orléans, as well as the king's mother, Marie de'Medici, both of whom became increasingly jealous of Richelieu's growing power. When they attempted a conspiracy against Richelieu, he successfully quashed it, and Louis XIII sent his mother into exile. In opposition to Marie's views, Richelieu favored an anti-Spanish, anti-Austrian policy. He made alliances with the Netherlands and German Protestant states, as well as with Sweden. Under Richelieu, France supported and heavily subsidized Gustavus II of Sweden in the Thirty Years' War, a policy that led to heavy taxation and depleted the French treasury, causing public outcry against Richelieu.

*Arts, Culture, Philosophy, and Science in the Age of
Richelieu*

Literature, science, theater, and Baroque art flourished
in the early part of the seventeenth century in France.
In this century, the French language enjoyed preemi-
nence in Europe, being the preferred tongue among
educated, civilized peoples. Famous Baroque painters
Nicolas Pouissin (1594–1665) and Claude Lorrain
(1600–1682) painted their most important landscapes
during this era. The first newspaper, *La Gazette,* was
published in 1631. In 1635, thanks largely to Richelieu's
patronage, the Académie Française was established,
paving the way for similar prestigious literary societies
in Russia and Germany. One of the first major acts of
the Académie was the compilation a dictionary of the
French language.

The early part of the seventeenth century also saw
major changes in conceptions of the structure of the
universe, and therefore a redirection in the current of
philosophical thought. The traditional Aristotelian geocentric notion of the universe, based on a cosmology of
a central Earth surrounded by concentric spheres con-
taining the planets and stars, had been challenged by
Copernicus in 1543. According to Copernicus, contrary
to Aristotelian belief, the Earth was in orbit and its stars
were, in fact, fixed. In 1632, Italian astronomer Galileo
Galilei (1564–1642), who had developed his own tele-
scopes and used them to observe the heavens, published his *Dialogue Concerning the Two Chief World
Systems,* a watershed in the continuing debate on Aristotelian theory. While Galileo's telescopic discoveries
did not precisely disprove the concept of a geocentric

universe, they added greatly to the argument for a heliocentric construction. Galileo had been reprimanded by the papacy for his potentially heretical arguments, such as 1610's *Sidereus Nuncus,* which included his letters on sunspots (an impossible phenomenon in an Earth-centered universe) and a biblical reinterpretation that favored heliocentric theory. But in 1633, one year after *Dialogue* was published, Galileo was brought before the Inquisition at Liège, forced to recant his Copernican views, and sent to live out his last years in exile.

Galileo's findings coincided with the writings of French philosopher René Descartes (1596–1650), who in 1637 published *A Discourse on Method,* the work credited with laying the foundations of modern philosophy. Descartes asserted that human beings are made up of distinct substances, the body and the mind. His *Discourse* ushered in a mode of thinking and science bound by doubt and based on evidence.

In this intellectual climate, the historical Cyrano de Bergerac thrived, for the work of Galileo and Descartes unexpectedly paved the way for a peculiar mode of literary expression: science fiction. In 1648, Bishop Godwin's *The Man in the Moone,* a story of a man who was carried to the moon on a machine ferried by a flock of birds, was published in a French edition. Cyrano was writing *L'Autre Monde (The Other World),* an eccentric, bawdy, and philosophical novel in which he described a "moon world," a place where all earthly notions about sex, love, religion, language, and so on were comically reversed, therefore casting traditional ideas into doubt. Undoubtedly Edmond Rostand had in mind the historical Cyrano's science fiction writings when crafting a scene in which Cyrano pretends to be a man sent from the moon. His Cyrano certainly captures the imagination of the historical Cyrano, as well as that of the consummate seventeenth-century Frenchman.

Belle Epoque *Paris*

To literary critics, the modern era in literature begins with the conclusion of World War I. This disastrous war was, in many ways, the death blow to a way of life that had existed in Europe for centuries. Dynasties crumbled, traditional relgious beliefs were cast into doubt, and millions upon millions of young men died. But in Western Europe just before the war came a period of general peace, merriment, and artistic energy known as the *belle epoque*, the beautiful era. People were enjoying the benefits of widespread prosperity and technological advancement. Automobiles, telephones, and other such inventions made life easier. Motion pictures made their first appearance as entertainment. People were excited by the wonderful possibilities of a new, modern century (before they came to realize the horrific nature of modern warfare). The arts flowered. Pablo Picasso (1881– 1973), who lived in Paris during this period, began painting his famous cubist works in 1908. Around the same time, Igor Stravinsky (1882–1971) composed the controversial, dissonant score for the ballet *The Rite of Spring,* which premiered in Paris in 1913 and featured the equally controversial, angular choreography of Vaslav Nijinksy (1890–1950). Playwrights such as Alfred Jarry (1873–1907), author of the strange farce *Ubu Roi* (1896), and symbolist Paul Claudel (1868-1955), author of *La Ville* (1890), created new dramatic genres. Theatrical productions in general were extremely popular in turn-of-the-twentieth-century Paris, and people of great and moderate means alike flocked to theaters. This trend benefited innovators like Jarry and Claudel as well as traditionalists like Edmond Rostand and Jules Renard. Rostand's lack of popular success after the appearance of *Cyrano de Bergerac* has much to do with rapid changes in society and literary taste. While *Cyrano*, with its unusual poetic structure and almost absurd hero, can be seen as somewhat experimental, Rostand's other plays were in a more traditional, nineteenth-century style not in keeping with the Parisian rage for modernity during the *belle epoque*.

CHRONOLOGY OF EDMOND ROSTAND'S LIFE AND WORK

1868: Edmond Rostand is born in Marseille, France.

1878: Begins study at the Marseille Lycée.

1884: Continues study at Collège Stanislas in Paris. His poetry begins to appear in the small magazine *Mireille*.

1886: Begins law studies.

1887: Awarded the Marseille Academy prize for his essay "Two Novelists of Provence: Honoré de Urfé and Émile Zola."

1888: Writes *Le Gant Rouge (The Red Glove)* in collaboration with Henry Lee. The play is presented at the Cluny Theater with little success.

1890: Marries the poet Rosemonde Gérard on April 8. *Les Musardises (The Idlers)*, a poetry collection dedicated to Rosemonde, is published, but sells few copies.

1891: *Les Deux Pierrots (The Two Pierrots)*, a one-act play in verse, is published, but not accepted by the Comédie-Française. First son, Maurice, born on May 25.

1894: *Les Romanesques (Romantics)* is performed at the Comédie-Française and awarded the Toirac Prize. Second son, Jean, born on October 30.

1895: *La Princesse Lointaine (The Princess Far Away)* is performed on April 5 at the Théâtre de la Renaissance.

1896: Begins writing *Cyrano de Bergerac* in April. Takes Dreyfus's side in the Dreyfus Affair.

1897: *La Samaritaine (The Woman of Samaria)* is performed on April 14 at the Théâtre de la Renaissance. On December 28, *Cyrano de Bergerac* is first perfomed, to instant acclaim, at the Porte Saint-Martin Theater.

1899: *Cyrano de Bergerac* concludes its first run of four hundred performances.

1900: *L'Aiglon (The Eaglet)* opens on March 15 at the Théâtre Sarah-Bernhardt. Rostand suffers from pulmonary congestion and retires to the Atlantic Pyrenees. The Legion of Honor is bestowed on him on July 14.

1901: Becomes the youngest writer ever admitted to the Académie Française.

1910: Writes *Le Bois Sacré (The Sacred Wood)*, a fragmentary parody of the Faust story. Publishes *Le Cantique de l'Aile (The Canticle of the Wing)*. *Chantecler (Chanticleer)* is performed on February 7, but receives poor reviews.

1913: *Cyrano* is revived at the Porte Saint-Martin Theater and celebrates its thousandth production in France.

1914: Refused entrance into the French army due to his poor health. Publishes *Le Vol de la Marseillaise (The Flight of the Marseillaise)*, a volume of patriotic poems.

1918: Six weeks after the armistice ending World War I, Rostand dies in Paris in December, due to an epidemic of the Spanish flu.

1921: *La Dernière Nuit de Don Juan (The Last Night of Don Juan)* is published posthumously and produced one year later. It is poorly received.

HISTORICAL CONTEXT OF
CYRANO DE BERGERAC

1617: Louis XIII is crowned king of France at the age of sixteen.

1618: Start of the Thirty Years' War. Richelieu is sent into exile in Avignon.

1619: The historical Cyrano de Bergerac is born Savinien Cyrano in Paris.

1620: Richelieu negotiates peace in France between rebelling nobles and the crown.

1621: Huguenots assemble at La Rochelle and declare a rebellion against Louis XIII.

1622: Richelieu becomes a cardinal. Cyrano's family moves to the small town of Bergerac.

1624: Cardinal Richelieu is appointed principal minister of France by Louis XIII. England declares war on Spain.

1626: Richelieu makes publishing works against religion or the state punishable by death. Louis XIII publishes an edict that condemns to death anyone who kills his adversary in a duel.

1627: Huguenots rise again to protect their freedom of worship. In science, Johannes Kepler compiles the *Rudolphine Tables*, which give the placement of 1,005 fixed stars.

1628: La Rochelle, defended by the Huguenots, falls to the French monarchy.

1629: The Spanish aid the Huguenots in a last act of resistance against the French crown.

1630: Cardinal Richelieu crushes a conspiracy against him led by Marie de' Medici and Gaston d'Orléans.

1632: Galileo publishes *Dialogue Concerning the Two Chief World Systems*.

1633: The Inquisition at Liège forces Galileo to retract his Copernican views.

1635: Beginning of France's intervention in the Thirty Years' War. The Académie Française is founded.

1637: Corneille's *Le Cid* is produced. Descartes publishes *A Discourse on Method*.

1638: Louis XIV is born.

1639: Savinien Cyrano is shot at the siege of Mouzon in Champagne.

1640: Savinien Cyrano is badly wounded at the siege of Arras.

1642: Death of Cardinal Richelieu. Mazarin succeeds him as minister. English Civil War begins.

1643: Louis XIII dies and is succeeded by Louis XIV.

1648: The Peace of Westphalia ends the Thirty Years' War. France gains Alsace.

1649: Savinien Cyrano writes *L'Autre Monde*, a three-volume work of early science fiction.

1654: Louis XIV crowned at Rheims.

1655: Savinien Cyrano dies in Sannois at the age of thirty-six, most likely of syphilis.

CYRANO DE BERGERAC

AUTHOR'S DEDICATION

It was to the soul of Cyrano that I wished to dedicate this poem.

But since his soul has passed into you, Coquelin, I dedicate my work to you.

E.R.

DRAMATIS PERSONÆ

CYRANO DE BERGERAC,
CHRISTIAN DE NEUVIL-
   LETTE,
THE COMTE DE GUICHE,
RAGUENEAU,
LE BRET,
CAPTAIN CARBON DE CAS-
   TEL–JALOUX,
THE CADETS,
LIGNIÈRE,
DE VALVERT,
A MARQUIS,
SECOND MARQUIS,
THIRD MARQUIS,
MONTFLEURY,
BELLEROSE,
JODELET,
CUIGY,
BRISSAILLE,

A BUSYBODY,
A MUSKETEER,
ANOTHER,
A SPANISH OFFICER,
A LIGHT GUARDSMAN,
THE DOORKEEPER,
A TRADESMAN,
HIS SON,
A PICKPOCKET,
A SPECTATOR,
A GUARD,
BERTRANDOU, THE FIFER,
THE CAPUCHIN,
TWO MUSICIANS,
THE POETS,
THE PASTRY-COOKS.

ROXANE,
SISTER MARTHA,

LISE,
MOTHER MARGARET DE
    JÉSUS,
SISTER CLAIRE,
THE ORANGE-GIRL,

THE DUENNA,
AN ACTRESS,
THE SOUBRETTE,
THE PAGES,
THE FLOWER-GIRL.

Cyrano de Bergerac

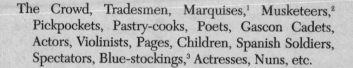

The Crowd, Tradesmen, Marquises,[1] Musketeers,[2] Pickpockets, Pastry-cooks, Poets, Gascon Cadets, Actors, Violinists, Pages, Children, Spanish Soldiers, Spectators, Blue-stockings,[3] Actresses, Nuns, etc.

(The first four acts in 1640; the fifth in 1655.)

First Act

A Performance at the Hôtel de Bourgogne.[4]

The hall of the Hôtel de Bourgogne in 1640. A sort of tennis court arranged and decorated for performances. The hall is oblong, seen diagonally, so that one of its sides forms the background, which runs from the first entrance on the right to the last entrance on the left, where it meets the stage, which is seen obliquely. This stage is provided with benches on each side, along the wings. The curtain is com-

posed of two pieces of tapestry which may be sepa-
rated. Above Harlequin's cloak are the royal arms.
High steps lead down from the platform to the floor.
On each side of these steps is the orchestra. Candles
serve as footlights. Two galleries along the side, one
above the other; the upper gallery is divided into
boxes. No seats in the parterre,[5] which is the actual
stage of the theatre; in the rear of this parterre, that
is to say, to the right, first entrance, are benches rising in tiers; and under a staircase which leads to the
upper seats, and of which only the beginning is visible, a sort of sideboard provided with little candelabra, vases of flowers, glasses, plates of cake, bottles,
etc. In the middle of the background, under the tier
of boxes, the entrance of the theatre. A large door,
which partly opens to let in the audience. On the
leaves of the door, as well as in several other places,
and above the sideboard, red posters on which are
the words "La Clorise."[6] When the curtain rises the
hall is half lighted and still empty, the chandeliers
are lowered in the middle of the parterre, waiting to
be lighted.

Scene I.

The Public, arriving little by little. Gentlemen, Tradesmen, Lackeys,[7] Pages, Pickpockets, the Doorkeeper,
etc.; then the Marquises, Cuigy, Brissaille, the
Orange-girl, the Violins, etc.

*(A sound of voices is heard behind the door; then a
Gentleman enters suddenly.)*

THE DOORKEEPER (*following him*).

    Holloa! Your fifteen pence!

THE GENTLEMAN.   I come in free.

THE DOORKEEPER.   Why?

THE GENTLEMAN.   I'm a guardsman of the Royal
    Household.

THE DOORKEEPER (*to another gentleman who has just
    come in*).

    And you?

SECOND GENTLEMAN.   Oh, no!

THE DOORKEEPER.   But—

SECOND GENTLEMAN.   I'm a musketeer!

FIRST GENTLEMAN (*to the second*).

    The play does not begin till two o'clock;

    The house is empty, let us try our foils.[8]

    (*They fence with the foils which they have brought.*)

A LACKEY (*entering*).   Pst—Flanquin!—

ANOTHER (*already in*).   Champagne?—

THE FIRST (*showing him games which he takes out of his
    doublet*).   Cards, dice.

(*Sits down on the ground.*)   Let us play.

THE SECOND (*same action*).

    Why, yes, my boy!

FIRST LACKEY (*taking from his pocket a candle end,
    which he lights and sets on the floor*).

    I've taken from my master

    A bit of candle.

A GUARD (*to a flower-girl who comes forward*).

    It is fine to come

    Before the lights are lit.

ONE OF THE FENCERS (*getting a stroke of the foil*).

    Touched!

ONE OF THE GAMESTERS.   Clubs!

THE GUARD (*pursuing the girl*).   A kiss!

THE FLOWER-GIRL (*breaking away*).

  We shall be seen.

THE GUARD (*dragging her into a dark corner*).

  No danger!

A MAN (*sitting on the floor, together with others who
      have brought eatables*).

  When one comes

  Before the play, one has a chance to eat.

A TRADESMAN (*escorting his son*).

  Let us wait here, my son.

A GAMBLER.   Aces!

A MAN (*taking a bottle of wine from under his cloak, and
      sitting down*).

  A drinker

  Should drink his Burgundy

(*drinks*)   at the Hôtel de Bourgogne.[9]

THE TRADESMAN (*to his son*).

  Would you not think it was some evil place?

    (*Points out the drinker with the end of his cane.*)

  Drinkers!

(*As they separate, one of the fencers pushes him over.*)

  Fighters!

            (*Falls among the card-players.*)

  Gamblers!

THE GUARD (*behind him, still struggling with the girl*).

  A kiss!

THE TRADESMAN (*drawing his son away quickly*).

  Good heavens!

  And just to think that in a hall like this

  They played Rotrou, my son!

THE YOUNG MAN.   And Corneille[10] too!

A BAND OF PAGES (*holding one another's hands, enter, singing and dancing*).

Tra la la la la la la la la la la lère.

THE DOORKEEPER (*severely, to the pages*).

No nonsense, boys!

FIRST PAGE (*with wounded dignity*). Oh, sir, what a suspicion!

(*Quickly to the second, as soon as the Doorkeeper has turned his back.*)

Have you some string?

THE SECOND. Yes, and a hook as well.

FIRST PAGE. From up above there we can fish for wigs.

A PICKPOCKET (*gathering several evil-looking men about him*).

And now, young rascals, come and take your lesson,
Since this will be your first attempt at thieving.

SECOND PAGE (*calling to other pages already in position in the upper galleries*).

Holloa! Have you your blow-guns?[11]

THIRD PAGE (*from up above*). Yes, and peas!
       (*Blows, and showers them with peas.*)

THE YOUNG MAN (*to his father*).

What is the play?

THE TRADESMAN. "Clorise."

THE YOUNG MAN. Whose work is it?

THE TRADESMAN. Monsieur Balthazar Baro's. 'Tis a piece!
          (*Walks off, taking his son's arm.*)

THE PICKPOCKET (*to his pupils*).

Cut off the lace upon the canons' robes!

ONE OF THE AUDIENCE (*to another, pointing out one of the upper seats*).

I sat there[12] on the first night of "The Cid"!

THE PICKPOCKET (*making the gesture of snatching*).
    Watches—

THE TRADESMAN (*returning, to his son*). You'll see the
    most distinguished actors—

THE PICKPOCKET (*making the gesture of pulling out with
    little stealthy jerks*).
    Handkerchiefs—

THE TRADESMAN.   Montfleury—

A MAN (*calling from the upper gallery*).   Light up the
    candles!

THE   TRADESMAN.   Bellerose, L'Épy, Beaupré, and
    Jodelet![13]

A PAGE (*in the parterre*).
    Ah, here's the Orange-girl!

THE ORANGE-GIRL.   Oranges, milk,
    Raspberry syrup, lemonade!
                    (*A noise at the door.*)

A FALSETTO VOICE.   Room, beasts!

A LACKEY (*in surprise*).
    Marquises—in the pit?

ANOTHER LACKEY.   Oh, for a moment!
                    (*Enter a little band of Marquises.*)

A MARQUIS (*seeing the hall empty*).
    How's this? Do we arrive like simple shopmen,
    Disturbing no one, treading on no toes?
    Ah, fie for shame!

(*Finds himself facing some other gentlemen who have
            come in a few moments before.*)
    Cuigy, Brissaille!
                    (*Great embracings.*)

CUIGY.   The faithful!
    Yes, we arrive even before the candles.

THE MARQUIS.   Tell me not of it. I'm in such a humor—
ANOTHER.   Cheer up, Marquis! Here the lamplighter
 comes!
THE HALL (*greeting the entrance of the lamplighter*).
 Ah!
(*Groups are formed around the candelabra, which he
 lights. A few people have taken their places in the
 galleries. Lignière enters the parterre, giving his arm
 to Christian de Neuvillette. Lignière is somewhat
 dishevelled, and looks dissipated, but distinguished.
 Christian is handsomely dressed, but rather behind the
 fashion, appears preoccupied, and looks at the boxes.*)

Scene II.

The Same; Christian, Lignière, then Ragueneau and Le
 Bret.

CUIGY.   Lignière!
BRISSAILLE (*smiling*).   Not drunk yet?
LIGNIÈRE (*aside to Christian*).   Shall I introduce you?
  (*Sign of assent from Christian.*)
 Baron de Neuvillette.
  (*Bows.*)
THE HALL (*hailing the ascent of the first lighted chande-
 lier*).   Ah!
CUIGY (*to Brissaille, looking at Christian*).
 Charming head!
FIRST MARQUIS (*who has heard*).
 Pooh!
LIGNIÈRE (*introducing them to Christian*). Messieurs de
 Cuigy, de Brissaille—

CHRISTIAN *(bowing)*.
  Delighted!
FIRST MARQUIS *(to the second)*.
  He's well enough, but not quite in the style.
LIGNIÈRE *(to Cuigy)*.
  He's just from the Touraine.
CHRISTIAN.   Yes, I have been
  Scarce twenty days in Paris. But to-morrow
  I join the guards, to serve with the Cadets.
FIRST MARQUIS *(looking at the people as they come into
    the boxes)*.
  There's Madame Aubry.
THE ORANGE-GIRL.   Oranges, milk!
THE VIOLINS *(tuning up)*.   La, la!
CUIGY *(to Christian indicating the hall, which is filling
    up)*.   A crowd!
CHRISTIAN.   Yes, quite.
FIRST MARQUIS.   All the fine world.
*(They name the women as they enter the boxes arrayed
    in all their finery. Exchange of bows and smiles.)*
SECOND MARQUIS.   Mesdames De Guémenée—
CUIGY.   Bois Dauphin—
FIRST MARQUIS.   Whom we loved—
BRISSAILLE.   De Chavigny—
SECOND MARQUIS.   Who plays with all our hearts.
LIGNIÈRE.   Monsieur de Corneille has come back from
    Rouen.
THE YOUNG MAN *(to his father)*.
  The Academy is there?
THE TRADESMAN.   Oh, yes! I see
  More than a few—Boudu, Boissat, Cureau,
  Porchères, Colomby, Bourzeys, and Bourdon:[14]
  All names that will not die; how fine it is!

FIRST MARQUIS.   Attention! Our blue-stockings take
 their places!
 Barthénoïde, Urimédonte, Félixe.
 Cassandacë.[15]

SECOND MARQUIS.   Heavens, what charming names!
 You know them all, Marquis?

FIRST MARQUIS.   I know them all.

LIGNIÈRE *(taking Christian aside)*.
 My friend, I came to-night to lend you aid;
 The lady comes not. Back to drink I go.

CHRISTIAN *(entreating)*.
 No! You, who tell me tales of town and court,
 Stay; you will know for whom I die of love!

THE FIRST VIOLIN *(rapping on his desk with his bow)*.
 Attention, sirs!

    (Raises his bow.)

THE ORANGE-GIRL.   Macaroons, lemonade!

CHRISTIAN.   I fear lest she be a coquette and witty.
 I dare not talk to her; I have no brains.
 The language that folk write and speak to-day
 Troubles me much. I'm but a timid soldier.
 She's always there—to the right, the empty box.

LIGNIÈRE *(moving as if to start)*.   I go.

CHRISTIAN *(still holding him back)*.   No, stay!

LIGNIÈRE.   I cannot. D'Assoucy[16]
 Waits for me at the tavern. Here 'tis thirsty.

THE ORANGE-GIRL *(passing him with a tray)*.   Orange
 juice?

LIGNIÈRE.   No!

THE ORANGE-GIRL.   Milk?

LIGNIÈRE.   Pooh!

THE ORANGE-GIRL.   Muscatel?

LIGNIÈRE.   Stop!

(to Christian) I'll stay a bit. Let's try your muscatel.[17]
          (Sits down by the sideboard.
          The girl pours out his muscatel.)

CRIES IN THE CROWD *(on the entrance of a little man,*
     rather fat and very beaming).

     Ah, Ragueneau!

LIGNIÈRE *(to Christian)*. Ragueneau, the pastry-cook.

RAGUENEAU *(dressed in the Sunday costume of a pastry-*
     cook, quickly advancing towards Lignière).

     Sir, have you seen Monsieur de Cyrano?

LIGNIÈRE *(introducing Ragueneau to Christian).*

     The pastry-cook of actors and of poets!

RAGUENEAU *(in confusion).*

     You honor me too much—

LIGNIÈRE.   Be still, Mæcenas!

RAGUENEAU.   These gentlemen are served by me—

LIGNIÈRE.   On credit.

     He is himself a poet—

RAGUENEAU.   So they say.

LIGNIÈRE.   Crazy on verse.

RAGUENEAU.   'Tis true that for an ode—

LIGNIÈRE.   You'd give a tart.

RAGUENEAU.   Oh, just a little one!

LIGNIÈRE.   He would disclaim it— And for a triolet[18]

     Would you not give—

RAGUENEAU.   Some rolls!

LIGNIÈRE *(severely)*.   Milk-rolls, of course.

     You like the theatre, then?

RAGUENEAU.   I idolize it!

LIGNIÈRE.   You buy your theatre-tickets with your
     cakes.

     Your place to-day among us cost how much?

RAGUENEAU. Four cream-puffs, fifteen patties (*looks around on every side*)—I'm astonished!
Monsieur de Cyrano has not arrived?

LIGNIÈRE. But why?

RAGUENEAU. Montfleury plays!

LIGNIÈRE. 'Tis true, this barrel
Will play for us to-night the role of Phédon.
But what cares Cyrano?

RAGUENEAU. You do not know?
Montfleury, whom he hates, sirs, he forbade
To appear upon the stage for a whole month.

LIGNIÈRE (*who has reached his fourth glass*).
Well, then?

RAGUENEAU. Montfleury plays.

CUIGY (*who has approached with his group of friends*).
He cannot stop him.

RAGUENEAU. Oh! Oh! I've come to see.

FIRST MARQUIS. Who is this man,
This Cyrano?

CUIGY. A lad well skilled in sword-play.

SECOND MARQUIS. Noble?

CUIGY. Enough. In the Guards; a Cadet
(*Pointing out a gentleman going to and fro in the hall,
as if looking for some one.*)
His friend Le Bret can tell you.
(*Calls.*) Oh, Le Bret!
(*Le Bret comes toward them.*)
You look for Bergerac?

LE BRET. Yes, I am anxious—

CUIGY. He is a man who's quite out of the common?

LE BRET (*affectionately*).
He is the choicest soul of mortal men.

RAGUENEAU.   A poet!

CUIGY.   Swordsman!

BRISSAILLE.   Doctor!

LE BRET.   And musician!

LIGNIÈRE.   And what a strange appearance he presents!

RAGUENEAU.   In truth, I think that Philippe de Champaigne,
    Solemn and grave, will never paint him for us;
    But with his strange, grotesque extravagances
    He would have lent to Jacques Callot, now dead,
    A swashbuckler, to place among his masks.
    His hat is triply plumed, his doublet puffed,
    His sword-point holds his cloak far out behind,
    Like the tail feathers of a strutting cock;
    Prouder than all the braves that Gascony[19]
    Has borne and e'er will cherish like a mother;
    He bears, projecting from his spreading ruff,
    A nose—ah, what a nose it is, my lords!
    To see one pass with such a nose as that
    You could but cry, "Oh, no! 'Tis magnified!"
    And then you smile and say, "He'll take it off,"
    But this Monsieur de Bergerac never does.

LE BRET (*shaking his head*).
    Let him that would remark on it beware!

RAGUENEAU (*proudly*).
    His blade's the half of the dread shears of Fate!

FIRST MARQUIS (*shrugging his shoulders*).
    He will not come.

RAGUENEAU.   He will—I bet a chicken
    Cooked à la Ragueneau!

THE MARQUIS (*smiling*).   Done!
    (*Noises of admiration in the hall. Roxane has just
    appeared in her box. She sits down in front, and her*

duenna takes her place in the rear. Christian, busy
paying the Orange-girl, does not see her.)

SECOND MARQUIS *(with little exclamations).*
  Ah, sirs, she is
  Terribly ravishing!
FIRST MARQUIS.   A blushing peach
  Smiling with strawberry lips!
SECOND MARQUIS.   And so refreshing,
  If you come near you catch cold in your heart.
CHRISTIAN *(raises his head, sees Roxane, and quickly*
    grasping Lignière by the arm).
  'Tis she!
LIGNIÈRE *(looking).*   Ah?
CHRISTIAN.   Yes, speak quick. I am afraid!
LIGNIÈRE *(swallowing his muscatel in little sips).*
  Madeleine Robin, called Roxane,—a wit
  And learned.
CHRISTIAN.   Alas!
LIGNIÈRE.   Free, orphan, and a cousin
  Of Cyrano—of whom we spoke.
(At this instant a very distinguished-looking nobleman,
  with the blue ribbon around his neck, enters the box,
    and stands talking for a moment with Roxane.)
CHRISTIAN *(starting).*   This man?—
LIGNIÈRE *(beginning to show the effects of drink, wink-*
    ing).
  Ha! ha! The Comte De Guiche, in love with her,—
  Married to Richelieu's niece,— would marry Roxane
  To a Monsieur de Valvert, old and dull,
  A vicomte, and obliging,— You know the way![20]
  She's not consented, but De Guiche has power;
  He well can persecute a simple girl.
  Besides, I have exposed his evil plan

In a song,—Ho, he should bear me a grudge!
The end was biting,—Listen,—
*(Gets up, staggering, and holding his glass aloft ready
to sing.)*

CHRISTIAN.   No, good night.

LIGNIÈRE.   You go?

CHRISTIAN.   To seek De Valvert.

LIGNIÈRE.   Have a care.
'Tis he will kill you!
(Indicating Roxane with the corner of his eye.)
Stay, they're looking at you.

CHRISTIAN.   'Tis true.

*(He remains lost in thought. The group of pickpockets
at this moment, seeing him with head in air and mouth
open, draws near him.)*

LIGNIÈRE.   I go; I'm thirsty. I'm expected
In the wine shops!
(Goes out in a zigzag course.)

LE BRET *(who has made the tour of the hall, returning
towards Ragueneau, with reassured voice).*
No Cyrano.

RAGUENEAU *(incredulously).*   And yet—

LE BRET.   I still have hopes he has not seen the poster.

THE HALL.   Begin! Begin!

Scene III.

The Same, without Lignière; De Guiche, Valvert, then
Montfleury.

A MARQUIS *(seeing De Guiche coming out of Roxane's
box and crossing the parterre, surrounded by ob-*

sequious gentlemen, the Vicomte de Valvert among them).

De Guiche has quite a court!

ANOTHER.   Pf!—Still a Gascon.[21]

THE FIRST.   A Gascon keen and cool.

That kind succeeds! Let us pay our respects.
(They go towards De Guiche.)

SECOND MARQUIS.   Beautiful ribbons!

What color, Comte De Guiche?
"Kiss-me-my-darling," or "Breast-of-the-doe"?

DE GUICHE.   The color's called "Sick Spaniard."

FIRST MARQUIS.   Then the color

Tells but the truth, for soon, thanks to your valor,
The Spaniard will fare very ill in Flanders.[22]

DE GUICHE.   I go upon the stage. You come?

(He turns towards the stage, followed by all the Marquises and gentlemen. He turns back and calls.)

Valvert!

CHRISTIAN *(watching and listening to them, starts when he hears this name).*

The vicomte! Ah, let me throw in his face—

(Puts his hand in his pocket and finds the hand of a thief about to rob him. Turns around.)

What?

THE PICKPOCKET.   Oh!

CHRISTIAN.   I want a glove!

THE PICKPOCKET *(with a piteous smile).*

You find a hand.
        (Changing his tone, quickly, and aside.)

Let go! I'll tell a secret—

CHRISTIAN *(still holding fast).*   What?

THE PICKPOCKET.   Lignière,

Who just left—

CHRISTIAN (*same action*).   Well?

THE PICKPOCKET.   —is near to his last hour.

    A song of his cut deep one of the great—

    A hundred men—I'm one—to-night are posted—

CHRISTIAN.   A hundred? And by whom?

THE PICKPOCKET.   A secret!

CHRISTIAN (*shrugging his shoulders*).   Oh!

THE PICKPOCKET (*with great dignity*).

    Professional confidence!

CHRISTIAN.   Where will they be?

THE PICKPOCKET.   Hard by the Porte de Nesle,²³ upon
    his way.

    Warn him!

CHRISTIAN (*at last letting go of the man's hand*).   But
    where to find him?

THE PICKPOCKET.   Go the rounds

    Of all the wine shops. Try the Golden Wine-press,

    The Pine Cone, or the Sign o' the Broken Belt,

    The Double Torch, the Funnels,—and in each

    Leave him a little note to give him warning.

CHRISTIAN.   I run. The scoundrels! 'Gainst one man a
    hundred!

        (*Looking at Roxane with love.*)

    Leave her!

(*At Valvert, with fury.*)

    And him! But Lignière I must save.

    (*Goes out on a run. De Guiche, the Vicomte, the
Marquises, and all the gentlemen have disappeared
behind the curtain to take their places on the stage
benches. The parterre is entirely filled. Not an empty
place in the galleries or the boxes.*)

THE HALL.   Begin!

A TRADESMAN (*whose wig flies away at the end of a*

string, fished up by a page in the upper gallery).
My wig!

CRIES OF JOY.   He's bald. Cheer for the pages!
Ha! ha! ha!

THE TRADESMAN *(furious and shaking his fist).*
Little rascal!

LAUGHTER AND SHOUTS *(beginning very loud and diminishing).*
Ha! ha! ha!

(Total silence.)

LE BRET *(astonished).*
This sudden silence?

(A spectator speaks to him aside).   Ah?

A SPECTATOR.   They say 'tis certain!

SCATTERING MURMURS. Hush! He appears? No! Yes!
In the latticed box.
The Cardinal![24] The Cardinal? 'Tis he!

A PAGE.   The devil! Now we must behave ourselves.
*(A rapping on the stage. Every one becomes
motionless. A pause.)*

THE VOICE OF A MARQUIS *(in the silence, behind the curtain).*
That candle should be snuffed!

ANOTHER MARQUIS *(thrusting his head out between the
curtains).*   A chair!

*(A chair is passed up over the heads of the crowd, from
hand to hand. The Marquis takes it and disappears,
after having thrown several kisses to the boxes.)*

A SPECTATOR.   Be still!

*(The three raps are heard. The curtain opens. Tableau.
The Marquises are seated at the sides in careless
attitudes. The background represents a pastoral scene,
painted in light colors. Four little crystal chandeliers
light the stage. The violins play softly.)*

LE BRET *(to Ragueneau, aside).*
    Montfleury will appear?
RAGUENEAU *(also aside).*   Yes, he begins.
LE BRET.   Cyrano is not there?
RAGUENEAU.   I've lost my bet.
LE BRET.   So much the better!
    *(The music of a shepherd's pipe is heard, and
Montfleury appears, very fat, in a shepherd's costume,
his hat decorated with roses and cocked over one ear.
    He is blowing on a pipe ornamented with ribbons.)*
THE PARTERRE *(applauding).* Bravo, Montfleury!
MONTFLEURY *(after bowing, playing the role of Phédon).*

        "Oh, happy he who in sweet solitude
        Becomes a willing exile from the Court;
        And who, when Zephyrus[25] gently breathed"—

A VOICE *(in the middle of the parterre).*
    Rascal, was't not for a month I warned you off?
    (Amazement. Every one turns around, murmurs.)
VARIOUS VOICES.   What is't?
            (People stand up in the boxes to look.)
CUIGY.   'Tis he!
LE BRET *(in alarm).*   Cyrano!
THE VOICE.   King of gluttons,
    Off from the stage at once!
ALL THE HALL *(in indignation).*   Oh!
MONTFLEURY.   But—
THE VOICE.   You baulk?
VARIOUS VOICES *(from the parterre and the boxes).*
    Enough! Hush! Play, Montfleury,—do not fear!
MONTFLEURY *(in a voice ill at ease).*

        "Oh, happy he who in sweet solitude"—

THE VOICE (*more threateningly*).
   Well, must I plant a forest on your shoulders,
   Monarch of scoundrels?
   (*A cane at the end of an arm springs out above the
               heads of the crowd.*)
MONTFLEURY (*his voice growing weaker and weaker*).
    "Happy he"—
             (*The cane is shaken.*)
THE VOICE.   Go!
THE PARTERRE.   Oh!
MONTFLEURY (*choking*).

        "Oh, happy he who"—

CYRANO (*rising from the parterre, standing on a chair,
   his arms crossed, his hat cocked, his moustache
   bristling, his nose terrible*).
   Ah, I shall grow angry!
       (*Sensation at his appearance.*)

Scene IV.

The Same; afterwards Bellerose and Jodelet.

MONTFLEURY (*to the Marquises*).
   Come to my aid, sirs!
A MARQUIS (*indifferently*).   Well, go on and act.
CYRANO.   Lump, if you act, I needs must punish you!
THE MARQUIS.   Hold!
CYRANO.   Let the Marquises sit quietly;
   Or else my cane may trifle with their ribbons!
ALL THE MARQUISES (*standing*).
   This is too much! Montfleury—

CYRANO.   Let him go;
   Or I shall clip his ears, and rip him up!
A VOICE.   But—
CYRANO.   Let him go!
ANOTHER VOICE.   And yet—
CYRANO.   'Tis not yet done?
  (Going through the motion of rolling up his sleeves.)
   Good! I approach the stage as 'twere a sideboard,
   To carve in slices this Italian sausage.
MONTFLEURY *(collecting all his dignity).*
   Your words to me insult the Comic Muse!
CYRANO *(very politely).*
   If this Muse, sir, to whom you are as naught,
   To meet you had the honor, mark my words,
   When she saw all your fat stupidity
   She'd use her sandals on you with a will!
THE PARTERRE.   Montfleury! Montfleury! Give Baro's
   play!
CYRANO *(to those who are shouting around him).*
   I beg of you, have pity on my scabbard;
   If you keep on it will yield up its blade!
        (The circle grows larger.)
THE CROWD *(drawing back).*   Holloa!
CYRANO *(to Montfleury).* Get off the stage!
THE CROWD *(drawing nearer and grumbling).*   Oh!
CYRANO *(turning around quickly).*   Who objects?
        (They draw back again.)
A VOICE *(singing in the background).*

        Monsieur de Cyrano
        Rules us with iron sway;
        But, though he says us no,
        Still "Clorise "they will play.

ALL THE HALL (*singing*).

     —Still "Clorise" they will play.

CYRANO.   If once again I hear you sing this song
    I'll slay you all.

A TRADESMAN.   You are not Samson yet!

CYRANO.   Will you, sir, kindly lend to me your jaw-
    bone?

A LADY (*in one of the boxes*).
    This is unheard of!

A NOBLEMAN.   It is scandalous!

A TRADESMAN.   It is vexatious!

A PAGE.   And this is amusement!

THE PARTERRE.   Ksss—Cyrano!—Montfleury!

CYRANO.   Silence, all!
      (*Shouts and cat-calls from the parterre.*)

CYRANO.   I order you straightway to hold your tongues;
    I send a general challenge to you all!
    Come on, young heroes, I will take your names,
    Each in his turn; I'll give to each his number!
    Come, who's the man who bravely heads the list?
    You, sir? No! You? No! Who is for a duel?
    I'll speed him with the honors which are due.
    Let all who wish to die now raise their hands.
                (*Silence.*)
    Shame will not let you see my naked blade?
    No name? No hand?— 'Tis well. I shall go on.
    (*Turning back towards the stage, where Montfleury
               waits in despair.*)
    Now! I desire to see the theatre healed
    Of this foul sore. If not—
    (*his hand on his sword*) —the lancet, then.

MONTFLEURY.   I—

CYRANO *(descends from his chair, sits down in the mid-*
dle of a circle which is formed around him, and
settles himself as if at home).

　I shall clap my hands three times, like this!
　You'll vanish at the third.

THE PARTERRE *(amused).*   Ah!

CYRANO *(clapping his hands).*   One!

MONTFLEURY.   I—

A VOICE *(from the boxes).*   Stay!

THE PARTERRE.   He'll stay—he will not—

MONTFLEURY.   I think, gentlemen—

CYRANO.   Two!

MONTFLEURY.   I am sure it would be better—

CYRANO.   Three!

　(Montfleury disappears as if through a trap door. A
burst of laughter, hisses, and hoots.)

THE HALL.   Coward! Come back!

CYRANO *(beaming, drops back in his chair and crosses*
his legs).

　Let him come, if he dare!

A TRADESMAN.   The spokesman of the troupe!
　　　　　(Bellerose advances and bows.)

THE BOXES.   Ah!—there's Bellerose!

BELLEROSE *(with elegance).*

　Most noble lords—

THE PARTERRE.   No! Jodelet!

JODELET *(comes forward, talking through his nose).*

　Pack of curs!

THE PARTERRE.   Oh! Bravo! Good enough! Bravo!

JODELET.   No bravos!

　The fat tragedian whose girth you love
　Felt—

THE PARTERRE.   He's a coward.

JODELET.   —that he should go out!

THE PARTERRE.   Let him come back!

SOME OF THE CROWD.   No!

OTHERS.   Yes!

A YOUNG MAN *(to Cyrano).*   But, sir, in short,
    What reason have you to hate Montfleury?

CYRANO *(graciously, still seated).*
    Young bantling,[26] I have two, and each alone
    Is quite enough: First, he's a wretched actor,
    Who mouths, and utters with a porter's grunts
    The lines which ought to fly away like birds;
    The second—is my secret.

THE OLD TRADESMAN *(behind him).*   But you rob us
    Of "Clorise," without scruples,— I object—

CYRANO *(turning his chair towards the Tradesman, re-*
      spectfully).
    Old mule, since Baro's verse is less than nothing I in-
      terrupt without regret!

THE BLUE-STOCKINGS *(in the boxes).*   Our Baro!
    My dear! How can he say it? Ah! Good heavens!

CYRANO *(turning his chair towards the boxes, gallantly).*
    Fair creatures, beam and blossom; be seneschals[27]
    Of dreams, and with a smile charm us to death.
    Inspire poetry—but judge it not!

BELLEROSE.   The money that must be returned?

CYRANO *(turning his chair towards the stage).*
    Bellerose,
    You have just spoken the first word of sense!
    I make no holes in Thespis'[28] honored cloak.
      (Gets up and tosses a bag on the stage.)
    Catch this purse on the fly and hold your tongue!

THE HALL *(dazed).*   Ah! Oh!

JODELET *(deftly catching the purse and trying its weight).*

    For this price, sir, I give you leave

    To come each night to stop "Clorise."

THE HALL.   Hoo! hoo!

JODELET.   We should be hissed together—

BELLEROSE.   Clear the hall!

(They begin to go out, while Cyrano looks on with a satisfied air. But the crowd soon stops to listen to the scene which ensues, and the exit ceases. The women in the boxes, who were already standing with their cloaks on, stop to listen and end by sitting down again.)

LE BRET *(to Cyrano).*   'Tis mad!

A BUSYBODY *(who has approached Cyrano).*

    Montfleury! It is scandalous!

    He is protected by the Duc de Candale.

    Have you a patron?

CYRANO.   No!

THE BUSYBODY.   You have not?

CYRANO.   No!

THE BUSYBODY.   What, no great lord to shield you with his name?

CYRANO *(with visible annoyance).*

    I said no twice. Must I, then, make it three?

    No; no protector—

(his hand on his sword)—but a good protectress!

THE BUSYBODY.   But you will leave the town?

CYRANO.   That all depends.

THE BUSYBODY.   The Duc de Candale's arm is long.

CYRANO.   Less long

    Than mine is—

(showing his sword)—when I give it this extension.

THE BUSYBODY.   You do not dream of trying—

CYRANO.   Yes, I do!
THE BUSYBODY.   But—
CYRANO.   Right about face, now!
THE BUSYBODY.   BUT—
CYRANO.   Right about!
   Or tell me why you are looking at my nose.
THE BUSYBODY (*in confusion*).   I—
CYRANO (*stepping up to him*).   What is strange about it?
THE BUSYBODY (*drawing back*).   You mistake—
CYRANO.   Is it, sir, soft and swinging, like a trunk?
THE BUSYBODY (*same action*). I did not—
CYRANO.   Or hooked, like an owl's beak?
THE BUSYBODY.   I—
CYRANO.   There's a wart upon it?
THE BUSYBODY.   But—
CYRANO.   Or a fly
   Walking along it slowly? What's so strange?
THE BUSYBODY.   Oh—
CYRANO.   Is't a freak of nature?
THE BUSYBODY.   But I knew
   Enough to keep my eyes from glancing at it.
CYRANO.   And, if you please, why should you not look
      at it?
THE BUSYBODY.   I—
CYRANO.   It disgusts you, then?
THE BUSYBODY.   Sir—
CYRANO.   Seems its color
   Unwholesome to you?
THE BUSYBODY.   Sir!
CYRANO.   Does its shape shock you?
THE BUSYBODY.   No, not at all!
CYRANO.   Why so disparaging?
   Perhaps you think it is a trifle large.

THE BUSYBODY (*stammering*).
  I think it small, quite small, a tiny one!
CYRANO.   What? Call it so absurd a name as that?
  Call my nose little?
THE BUSYBODY.   Heavens!
CYRANO.   My nose is huge!
  Poor flat nose, stupid snub nose, flat-head, learn
  'Tis an appendage I am proud to bear,
  Because a large nose is the unfailing sign
  Of a good man and kindly, generous,
  Courteous, full of courage and of wit;
  Such as I am, and such as you're forbidden
  Ever to dream yourself, poor good-for-naught!
  For the inglorious face above your collar,
  Which my hand now will find, is full as bare—
                    (*Boxes his ears.*)
THE BUSYBODY.   Oh!
CYRANO.   —of pride, of wit, of poetry, of art,
  Of all adornment, and in fine of nose—
                (*turns him about by the shoulders,
                    suiting the action to the word*)
  —As that my boot shall find below your backbone!
THE BUSYBODY (*escaping*).
  The Guard! Help! Help!
CYRANO.   My warning to the idlers
  Who find the middle of my face amusing;—
  And if the joker's noble, 'tis my custom
  To give to him before I let him go
  Steel and not leather, in front, and higher up.
DE GUICHE (*who has come down from the stage, with
      the Marquises*).
  He becomes tiresome!

THE VICOMTE DE VALVERT (*shrugging his shoulders*).
  He blows his trumpet!
DE GUICHE.   Will no one answer him?
THE VICOMTE.   No one? But wait!
  I shall fling at him now some of my wit!
(*Advances towards Cyrano, who is watching him, and
    takes his place in front of him with a silly air.*)
  You—your nose is—nose is—very large.
CYRANO (*gravely*).   Very!
THE VICOMTE (*smiling*).   Ha!
CYRANO (*imperturbable*).   That is all?
THE VICOMTE.   But—
CYRANO.   No, young man.
  That is somewhat too brief. You might say —Lord!—
  Many and many a thing, changing your tone,
  As for example these;—Aggressively:
  "Sir, had I such a nose I'd cut it off!"
  Friendly: "But it must dip into your cup.
  You should have made a goblet tall to drink from."
  Descriptive: " 'Tis a crag—a peak—a cape!
  I said a cape?—'tis a peninsula."
  Inquisitive: "To what use do you put
  This oblong sheath; is it a writing-case
  Or scissors-box?" Or, in a gracious tone:
  "Are you so fond of birds, that like a father
  You spend your time and thought to offer them
  This roosting-place to rest their little feet?"
  Quarrelsome: "Well, sir, when you smoke your pipe
  Can the smoke issue from your nose, without
  Some neighbor crying, 'the chimney is afire'?"
  Warning: "Be careful lest this weight drag down
  Your head, and stretch you prostrate on the ground."

Tenderly: "Have a small umbrella made,
For fear its color fade out in the sun."
Pedantic: "Sir, only the animal
Called by the poet Aristophanes[29]
'Hippocampelephantocámelos'
Should carry so much flesh and bone upon him!"
Cavalier: "Friend, is this peg in the fashion?
To hang one's hat on, it must be convenient."
Emphatic: "Magisterial nose, no wind
Could give thee all a cold, except the mistral."[30]
Dramatic: " 'Tis the Red Sea when it bleeds!"
Admiring: "What a sign for a perfumer!"
Poetic: "Is't a conch; are you a Triton?"[31]
Naïve: "When does one visit this great sight?"
Respectful: "Let me, sir, pay my respects.
This might be called fronting upon the street."
Countrified: "That's a nose that is a nose!
A giant turnip or a baby melon!"
Or military: "Guard against cavalry!"
Practical: "Will you put it in a raffle?
It surely, sir, would be the winning number!"
Or parodying Pyramus,[32] with a sob:
"There is the nose that ruins the symmetry
Of its master's features; the traitor blushes for it."
My friend, that is about what you'd have said
If you had had some learning or some wit;
But wit, oh! most forlorn of human creatures,
You never had a bit of; as for letters
You only have the four that spell out "Fool"!
Moreover, had you owned the imagination
Needed to give you power, before this hall,
To offer me these mad jests—all of them—
You would not even have pronounced the quarter

O' the half of one's beginning, for I myself
Offer them to myself with dash enough,
But suffer no one else to say them to me.

DE GUICHE (*trying to lead away the dazed vicomte*)
Vicomte, leave off!

THE VICOMTE (*choking*).   These great and lofty airs!
A rustic, who—who—even wears no gloves,
And goes about without a single ribbon.

CYRANO.   It is my character that I adorn.
I do not deck me like a popinjay;[33]
But though less foppish, I am better dressed:
I would not sally forth, through carelessness,
With an insult ill wiped out, or with my conscience
Sallow with sleep still lingering in its eyes,
Honor in rags, or scruples dressed in mourning.
But I go out with all upon me shining,
With liberty and freedom for my plume,
Not a mere upright figure;—'tis my soul
That I thus hold erect as if with stays,
And decked with daring deeds instead of ribbons,
Twirling my wit as it were my moustache,
The while I pass among the crowd, I make
The truth ring out like spurs.

THE VICOMTE.   But, sir—

CYRANO.   I have
No gloves?—A pity!—I had just one left,
One of a worn-out pair!—which troubled me!
I left it recently in some one's face.

THE VICOMTE.   Knave, rascal, booby, flatfoot, scum o'
the earth!

CYRANO (*taking off his hat and bowing as if the Vicomte
had just introduced himself*).
Ah? And I—Cyrano-Savinien-Hercule de Bergerac.

(*Laughter.*)

THE VICOMTE (*in a temper*).   Buffoon!

CYRANO (*giving a cry like one who feels a sudden pain*).
   Oh!

THE VICOMTE (*who was going off, turning about*).
   What's he saying now?

CYRANO (*with grimaces of pain*).   I must
   Shake it, because it falls asleep—the fault
   Of leaving it long idle—

THE VICOMTE.   What's the matter?

CYRANO.   My sword-blade tingles!

THE VICOMTE (*drawing his own sword*).
   Very well, come on!

CYRANO.   I shall give you a charming little stroke.

THE VICOMTE (*with disdain*).   Poet!—

CYRANO.   A poet, yes! and such a one,
   That, while I fence with you, I'll improvise
   A ballade[34] for you.

THE VICOMTE.   A ballade?

CYRANO.   I suppose
   You do not e'en imagine what that is?

THE VICOMTE.   But—

CYRANO (*as if reciting a lesson*).
   The ballade, then, is made up of three stanzas,
   Of eight lines—

THE VICOMTE (*shuffling his feet*).   Oh!

CYRANO (*continuing*). And a refrain of four.

THE VICOMTE.   You—

CYRANO.   I'll make one and fight you, both at once.
   And at the last verse touch you, sir.

THE VICOMTE.   No!

CYRANO.   No?

The ballade of Monsieur de Bergerac's duel
At the Hôtel de Bourgogne with a booby.

THE VICOMTE.   What is that, if you please?
CYRANO.   That is the title.
THE HALL (*excited to the highest pitch*).
    In place!—No noise!—In line!—This is amusing.
(*Tableau. A circle of curious onlookers in the parterre,
    the Marquises and the Officers mixed in with the
    Tradesmen and common people. The Pages climb on
people's shoulders to see better. All the women stand
    up in the boxes. To the right De Guiche and
        his gentlemen. To the left Le Bret,
            Ragueneau, Cuigy, etc.*)
CYRANO (*closing his eyes for a moment*).
    Wait, let me choose my rhymes—I have them now.

    My hat I toss lightly away;
    From my shoulders I slowly let fall
    The cloak which conceals my array,
    And my sword from my scabbard I call,
    Like Céladon,[35] graceful and tall,
    Like Scaramouche,[36] quick hand and brain,—
    And I warn you, my friend, once for all,
    I shall thrust when I end the refrain.

(*The swords meet.*)

    You were rash thus to join in the fray;
    Like a fowl I shall carve you up small,
    Your ribs 'neath your doublet so gay,
    Your breast, where the blue ribbons fall,
    Ding dong! ring your bright trappings all;
    My point flits like a fly on the pane,

As I clearly announce to the hall
I shall thrust when I end the refrain.

I need one more rhyme for "array"—
You give ground, you turn white as the wall,—
And so lend me the word "runaway."
There! you have let your point fall
As I parry your best lunge of all;
I begin a new line, the end's plain,
Your skewer hold tight, lest it fall.
I shall thrust when I end the refrain.

(Announces solemnly.)

REFRAIN.

Prince, on the Lord you must call!
I gain ground, I advance once again,
I feint,[37] I lunge. *(Lunging.)* There! that is all!

(The Vicomte staggers. Cyrano salutes.)

For I thrust as I end the refrain.

*(Shouts. Applause in the boxes. Flowers and
handkerchiefs are thrown. The Officers surround
Cyrano and congratulate him. Ragueneau dances with
enthusiasm. Le Bret is dizzy with joy. The Vicomte's
friends hold him up and lead him away.)*

THE CROWD *(in one long cry).*   Ah!
A LIGHT GUARDSMAN.   Superb!
A WOMAN.   A pretty stroke!
RAGUENEAU.   Magnificent!
A MARQUIS.   Something quite new!
LE BRET.   Mad folly!
VOICES *(in the confusion about Cyrano).*

Compliments,
Congratulations, bravo!

VOICE OF A WOMAN.   He's a hero!

A MUSKETEER (*advancing quickly toward Cyrano with outstretched hands*).

Will you allow me, sir?—'Twas right well done,
And these are things I think I understand;
Besides, I have expressed my joy by stamping!
(*Withdraws.*)

CYRANO (*to Cuigy*). Who is this gentleman?

CUIGY.   He's D'Artagnan![38]

LE BRET (*to Cyrano, taking him by the arm*).

Come, let us talk—

CYRANO.   Let the crowd go out first.
(*To Bellerose.*)   May I wait?

BELLEROSE (*respectfully*).   Certainly!
(*Shouts are heard without.*)

JODELET (*after looking out*).   They hiss Montfleury!

BELLEROSE (*solemnly*).   "Sic transit"[39]—

(*Changing his tone, to the doorkeeper and the candle-snuffer.*) Sweep. Close up. But leave the lights.
We shall return when we have had our supper,
For a rehearsal of to-morrow's farce.
(*Jodelet and Bellerose go out, after low bows to Cyrano.*)

THE DOORKEEPER (*to Cyrano*).   You do not dine?

CYRANO. I?—No!

LE BRET (*to Cyrano*).   Because?

CYRANO (*proudly*).   Because—
(*Changing his tone when he sees that the Doorkeeper has gone.*)
I have no money!

LE BRET (*making the gesture of throwing a bag*).
What! the bag of crowns?

CYRANO.   Inheritance, in one day thou art spent!

LE BRET.   How will you live this month, then?

CYRANO.   Naught is left.

LE BRET.   What folly 'twas to throw away the bag!

CYRANO.   But what a stroke!

THE ORANGE-GIRL (*coughing behind her little counter*).
    Hum! hum!

(*Cyrano and Le Bret turn about. She advances timidly.*)
    To see you fasting—
    It breaks my heart.

(*Showing the sideboard.*)   I have all that is needed.

(*With enthusiasm.*) Take what you wish!

CYRANO (*taking off his hat*).   My Gascon pride forbids
    me,
    My child, to take one dainty from your hands,
    And yet I fear that this may cause you pain,
    And so I shall accept—
    (*goes to the sideboard and chooses*)—oh, nothing
    much!
    A grape—

(*She starts to give him the bunch; he picks one grape.*)
    But one! This glass of water!

(*She starts to pour in some wine; he stops her.*)   Clear!
    And half a macaroon!
    (*He returns the other half.*)

LE BRET.   But this is foolish!

THE ORANGE-GIRL.   Oh, something more!

CYRANO.   Why, yes, your hand to kiss!
    (*He kisses the hand which she holds out, as he would
                the hand of a princess.*)

THE ORANGE-GIRL.   I thank you, sir.

(*She courtesies.*)   Good night!
                        (*She goes out.*)

Scene V.

Cyrano, Le Bret, then the Doorkeeper.

CYRANO *(to Le Bret)*. Talk, I will listen.
  *(He takes his place before the sideboard, arranging
          before him the macaroon,)*
  Dinner.
(the glass of water,)   Drink!
(the grape.)   Sweets!
(He sits down.)   There, I sit down at table!
  Ah, friend, I was unconscionably hungry!
(Eating.)   You said?
LE BRET.   That these fools, with their warlike airs,
  Will spoil your wit if you consort with them;
  Consult men of good sense, and so find out
  The effect of your mad sally.
CYRANO *(finishing his macaroon.)*   It was huge.
LE BRET.   The Cardinal—
CYRANO *(beaming)*.   So the Cardinal was there?
LE BRET   —must have esteemed it—
CYRANO.   Quite original!
LE BRET.   Yet—
CYRANO.   He's an author. It cannot displease him
  If some one come to spoil a rival's work.
LE BRET.   You'll have too many enemies against you!
CYRANO *(attacking the grape)*.
  About how many have I made to-night?
LE BRET.   Without the women, forty-eight.
CYRANO.   Come, count!
LE BRET.   De Guiche, Montfleury, Valvert, and the
    Tradesman;
  The Academy and Baro—

CYRANO.   That's enough.
  You greatly please me!
LE BRET.   But this mode of life
  Where will it lead you? And what is your plan?
CYRANO.   I wandered in a maze; too many courses,
  And too bewildering, there were to choose.
  I've chosen—
LE BRET.   What?
CYRANO.   Oh, far the simplest one:
  I have resolved in all things to excel!
LE BRET (*shrugging his shoulders.*)
  So be it. But the reason of your hatred
  For Montfleury, the real one!
CYRANO (*getting up*).   This Silenus,[40]
  Who cannot reach the centre of his paunch,
  Thinks himself still a charmer of the women;
  And while he plays his part and mouths his words
  Casts glances at them with his fishy eyes!
  Him have I hated since one night he let
  His gaze rest on her—Oh, I seemed to see
  Upon a flower fair a great slug crawling.
LE BRET (*amazed*).
  What? What? And can it be—
CYRANO (*with a bitter smile*). That I should love?—
         (*Changing his tone and seriously.*)
  I love.
LE BRET.   And may I know? You never told me.
CYRANO.   Whom I love? Think, it is forbidden me
  To dream of love from e'en the most ill-favored—
  This nose, which goes before me half a mile!—
  And so whom do I love?—the answer's plain!
  I love—it is absurd—the very fairest!
LE BRET.   The fairest?

CYRANO.   Yes. In short, in the whole world;
   The most consummate charms,—
(with great dejection) —the fairest hair!
LE BRET.   Heavens, who is this woman?
CYRANO.   A mortal danger,
   Without intention; charming, without thought;
   A trap by nature set, a damask rose
   In which, close hid in ambush, Love is lurking!
   He who has known her smile has known perfection.
   Her grace is all unconscious; she sums up
   The whole of heaven in a single movement;
   And, Venus, thou couldst never mount thy shell,
   Nor thou, Diana, walk the leafy forests,
   As she mounts in her chair and walks these streets!
LE BRET.   I understand. 'Tis clear!
CYRANO.   'Tis quite transparent!
LE BRET.   Your cousin Magdeleine Robin?
CYRANO.   Yes, Roxane.
LE BRET.   Well, that is for the best. You love her? Tell her!
   You won great glory in her eyes to-day!
CYRANO.   Look at me, friend, and tell me what fond
      hopes
   This great protuberance could ever leave me?
   Oh! I have no illusions!—By the gods,
   Sometimes I soften, on an evening clear;
   I seek some green spot, when the hour is sweet,
   I scent the Spring with my poor monstrous nose.
   'Neath the moon's silver beams my gaze will follow
   Some woman passing on her lover's arm,
   And then I think I too should like to walk,
   With sweetheart on my arm, in the fair moonlight.
   My fancy rises, I forget,—and then
   I see my profile's shadow on the wall!

LE BRET (*with emotion*).   My friend!—

CYRANO.   My friend, I have my gloomy hours,
Knowing myself so ugly, and sometimes,
When quite alone—

LE BRET (*quickly taking his hand*).   You weep?

CYRANO.   Ah, never that!
No, that would be too ugly, if along
This monstrous nose a tear should trickle down!
I'll not permit, so long as I am master,
That such gross ugliness contaminate
The grace divine of tears! For, mark you well,
There's nothing more sublime on earth than tears;
I would not have one put to ridicule
By me, the while my plight should raise a laugh.

LE BRET.   Be not so mad! For love is naught but luck!

CYRANO (*shaking his head*).
No, I love Cleopatra. Am I Cæsar?[41]
I worship Berenice. Am I Titus?[42]

LE BRET.   But your wit! Your courage!— This poor child,
Who offered you just now this modest meal,—
Her eyes, you plainly saw, misliked you not!

CYRANO (*struck by the idea*).   That is the truth!

LE BRET.   Well, then; Roxane herself
Grew pale watching your duel.

CYRANO.   She grew pale?

LE BRET.   Her heart and mind already are much
moved.
Dare, tell her, so that—

CYRANO.   She'll laugh in my face!
No! 'Tis the one thing in the world I fear.

THE DOORKEEPER (*introducing some one to Cyrano*).
Sir, you are asked for.

CYRANO (*seeing the duenna*).[43]   Heavens! her duenna!

Scene VI.

Cyrano, Le Bret, the Duenna.

THE DUENNA (*with a profound bow*).
  Some one would be informed by her brave cousin
  Where one can see him secretly.
CYRANO (*in amazement*).   See me?
THE DUENNA (*with a courtesy*).
  See you. Some one has things to tell you.
CYRANO.   Things?
THE DUENNA (*with another courtesy*).   Yes.
CYRANO (*staggering*).   Heavens!
THE DUENNA.   To-morrow, at the blush of dawn,
  Some one will go to hear mass at Saint-Roch.
CYRANO (*leaning on Le Bret*).   Heavens!
THE DUENNA.   And after, where can some one stop
  For a short talk?
CYRANO (*delighted*).   Where—I—but—Lord—
THE DUENNA.   Speak quick.
CYRANO.   I'm thinking—
THE DUENNA.   Where?
CYRANO.   Ragueneau's, the pastry-cook's.
THE DUENNA.   Where?
CYRANO.   On the Rue—Ah, God! St. Honoré.
THE DUENNA (*retiring*).   She'll go, be there, at seven
    o'clock.
CYRANO. I shall!

Scene VII.

Cyrano, Le Bret, afterwards the Actors and Actresses,
  Cuigy, Brissaille, Lignière, the Doorkeeper, the Violins.

CYRANO (*falling into Le Bret's arms*).
  From her—for me—a meeting.
LE BRET.   You are sad
  No more?
CYRANO.   At least, she knows that I exist.
LE BRET.   And now you will be calm?
CYRANO (*beside himself*).   And now—and now—
  I shall be full of frenzy and of thunders!
  I want a regiment to put to rout!
  I've ten hearts; twenty arms; 'tis not enough
  To hew down dwarfs,—
(*shouts at the top of his voice*)—giants are what I want!
(*For the past moment, shadows of Actors and Actresses
    have been moving about on the stage in the
background and whispering; the rehearsal begins. The
    violins have resumed their places.*)
A VOICE (*from the stage*).
  Eh! down there! quiet! this is a rehearsal!
CYRANO (*smiling*).   We go!
  (*He starts to withdraw; by the great door in the
background enter Cuigy, Brissaille, and several Officers,
    who are holding up Lignière, now very drunk.*)
CUIGY.   Cyrano!
CYRANO.   What?
CUIGY.   A heavy load
  We bring you.
CYRANO (*recognizing him*). Lignière—what has happened to you?
CUIGY.   He's looking for you!
BRISSAILLE.   He cannot go home!
CYRANO.   Why?
LIGNIÈRE (*with a thick voice, showing him a crumpled
    note*).

This letter warns me—a hundred men against me—
Because—my song—great danger threatens me—
The Porte de Nesle—I pass it on my way—
Let me go with you—sleep under your roof!

CYRANO.   You said a hundred. You shall sleep at home!

LIGNIÈRE (*alarmed*).   But—

CYRANO (*with a terrible voice, showing him the lighted
    lantern, which the doorkeeper swings, while he
    listens with curiosity to the conversation*).   Take
    this lantern!—

        (*Lignière hurriedly seizes the lantern.*)

    March! I swear to you
    That it is I shall shelter you to-night!—
(*To the Officers.*)   Follow, but hold your distance,—be
    my seconds!

CUIGY.   A hundred men—

CYRANO.   To-night I want no less!

(*The Actors and Actresses who have come down from
    the stage approach in their various costumes.*)

LE BRET.   But why should you protect—

CYRANO.   Hear Le Bret scold!

LE BRET.   —this common drunkard?

CYRANO (*tapping Lignière on the shoulder*).
    Just because this drunkard,
    This tun of muscatel, this cask of brandy,
    One day performed a wholly charming deed;
    For as he left the mass, seeing his sweetheart,
    After the custom, take the holy water,—
    Though he flees water,—hastened to the font,
    Leaned over it, and straightway drank it all!

AN ACTRESS (*in soubrette costume.*)[44]
    Now that was fine!

CYRANO.   And was it not, my dear?

THE ACTRESS *(to the others).*

But why are there a hundred 'gainst one poet?

CYRANO.   Forward!—

(To the Officers).   And you, sirs, when you see me charge,

Give me no help, whatever be the danger.

ANOTHER ACTRESS *(jumping down from the stage).*

Oh, I am coming!—

CYRANO.   Come—

ANOTHER *(also jumping down, to an old actor).*

And you, Cassandra?

CYRANO.   Come all, Leander, Isabelle, the Doctor,—

All! You shall join, oh pleasant madcap throng,

Italian farce unto this Spanish drama,

And o'er its thunder jingling antic noise

Hang bells around it, like a tambourine!

ALL THE WOMEN *(jumping with joy).*   Bravo! A cape!

A cloak, quick!

JODELET.   Come along!

CYRANO *(to the Violins).*

Now, Violins, you'll play a tune for us!

(The Violins join the parade which is forming. Lighted candles are taken from the footlights and distributed. It becomes a torchlight procession.)

Bravo! Women in costume, officers,

And twenty paces to the front—

(takes his place as he speaks) —myself

Alone, beneath the plume by glory placed,

Full proud as Scipio[45] three times Nasica!

'Tis understood? No one to lend a hand!

Ready? One, two, three! Porter, clear the way!

(The doorkeeper opens both leaves of the door. A picturesque moonlit corner of old Paris appears.)

Ah! Paris seems almost dissolved in haze:
The moonlight falls over the slanting roofs;
A charming frame makes ready for the scene.
There, 'neath its wreathing mists, the river Seine,[46]
Like a mysterious and magic mirror,
Shimmers,—and you shall see what you shall see.

ALL.   On to the Porte de Nesle!

CYRANO *(standing on the threshold)*.   The Porte de
    Nesle!

    (Turning, before going out, to the Soubrette.)
Did you not ask me why, mademoiselle,
Against one poet five-score men are set?
    (Draws his sword and concludes placidly.)
Because 'tis known he is a friend of mine.

*(He goes out. The procession—Lignière zigzagging
at the head, then the Actresses, taking the Officers'
arms, then the Actors frolicking—starts on its
midnight march to the music of the Violins,
and the flaming light of the candles.)*

CURTAIN.

Second Act

The Poet's Cook-Shop.

*The shop of Ragueneau, baker and pastry-cook, a large
establishment at the corner of the Rue Saint-Honoré
and the Rue de l'Arbre Sec, a general view of which,
gray in the first light of dawn, is seen in the background through the glass panels of the door. To the
left, first entrance, there is a counter, and over it a
wrought-iron canopy, to which are hung white pea-*

cocks, ducks, and geese. In great china vases there are tall bouquets of common flowers, principally yellow sunflowers. On the same side, second entrance, there is a huge fireplace, in front of which, between large andirons, each of which supports a little saucepan, the roasts are dripping into pans. To the right, at the first entrance, a door. At the second entrance a staircase leading to a small room in a sort of loft, the interior of the room being visible through open blinds; a table is set there, lit by a little Flemish candlestick; it is a kind of private dining-room. A wooden gallery, extending from the head of the stairs, seems to lead to other similar small rooms. In the middle of the cook-shop an iron ring, which may be lowered by means of a cord, and upon which heads of large game are hanging, makes a sort of chandelier. The ovens, in the shadow under the staircase, are glowing. The coppers glisten. The spits are turning. There are great piles of fancy dishes all around. Hams hang from their hooks. It is the morning baking. There is a bustle of frightened scullions, tall cooks, and little knife-boys. Their caps bristle with chicken feathers or guinea fowls' wings. Rows of cream puffs and collections of fancy cakes are brought in on iron trays and wicker stands. Some of the tables are covered with cakes and other dishes. Others are surrounded with chairs, waiting for customers. A smaller table, in one corner, is hidden under a mass of papers. When the curtain rises Ragueneau is seated there, writing.

Scene I.

Ragueneau, the Pastry-cooks, afterwards Lise. Ragueneau, at the little table, is writing with an inspired air, and counting on his fingers.

FIRST PASTRY-COOK (*with a plate*).
   Puff paste!
SECOND PASTRY-COOK (*with a dish*).   And candied fruits!
THIRD PASTRY-COOK (*with a roast decorated with feathers*).
   A peacock!
FOURTH PASTRY-COOK (*with a plate of cakes*).   Sweetmeats!
FIFTH PASTRY-COOK (*with a sort of pan*).
   Fillet of beef with sauce!
RAGUENEAU (*stopping his writing and raising his head*).
   The silver light
   Of dawn already glistens on the coppers!
   Smother the god that sings in thee, Ragueneau!
   The lute's hour comes—this is the hour of ovens!
            (*Gets up,—to a cook.*)
   Lengthen this sauce for me, it is too short.
THE COOK.   How much?
RAGUENEAU.   Three feet.
                  (*Goes in.*)
FIRST PASTRY-COOK.   The patty!
SECOND PASTRY-COOK.   And the tart!
RAGUENEAU (*in front of the fireplace*).
   Depart, my muse, for fear thy charming eyes
   Should be made red by all this faggot smoke!
(*To a pastry-cook, showing him some loaves of bread.*)
   You've split these loaves quite wrong, for in the middle
   Goes the cæsura—between the hemistiches!
   (*To another, showing him an unfinished pasty.*)

You need a roof upon this pie-crust palace—
(To a young apprentice seated on the ground, who is putting fowls on a spit.)
And you upon this endless spit should put
The modest chicken, and the turkey proud,
Alternately, my son, as old Malherbe
Arranged the long lines with the shorter ones;
And turn the roasts before the fire in strophes.

ANOTHER APPRENTICE *(coming forward with a platter covered with a napkin).*
Master, with thought of you I have prepared
This, which I hope will please you.
(Uncovers the platter, and shows a great lyre of pastry.)

RAGUENEAU *(dazzled).*   Ah! A lyre!

THE APPRENTICE.   'Tis made of puff paste.

RAGUENEAU *(with emotion).*   And with candied fruits?

THE APPRENTICE.   And look! the strings are made all of spun sugar.

RAGUENEAU *(giving him money).*   Go, drink my health!
(Seeing Lise coming in.) Hush, there's my wife!
    Make off!
And hide this money!
(To Lise, with an air of annoyance, showing her the lyre.)   Is't not fine?

LISE.   Absurd!
       (Puts a pile of paper bags on the counter.)

RAGUENEAU.   Bags? Good—I thank you.
(Looks at them.) Heavens! My honored books—
    The verses of my friends! Torn! Cut to pieces!
    To make up bags wherein to carry biscuits—
    Ah! Orpheus and the Mænads[1] you repeat!

LISE *(drily).*   And have I not the right to put to use

The only thing they ever leave for payment—
Your wretched scribblers of uneven lines?

RAGUENEAU. Ant!—do not thus insult divine
grasshoppers.

LISE.   My dear, before these folk became your friends
You did not call me Mænad—nor yet ant!

RAGUENEAU.   To do such things to poetry!

LISE. Naught else!

RAGUENEAU.   What would you then have done had it
been prose?

Scene II.

The Same, and Two Children who have just come into
the Shop.

RAGUENEAU.   What do you wish, my dears?

FIRST CHILD.   Three patties, please.

RAGUENEAU (*waiting on them*).
There, nicely done,—and hot.

SECOND CHILD.   And, if you please,
Wrap them up for us.

RAGUENEAU (*aside*).   Ah! One of my bags!
(*To the children.*)   Wrap them up for you? Certainly,
my dears.
(*Takes a bag, and just as he is putting the patties into
it, reads:*)
"*Ulysses, when he left Penelope*"—
Not that one!
(*Puts it aside and takes another. Just as he is putting the
patties in, reads:*) "*Bright-haired Phœbus*"—
Nor yet that!

(Same action.)

LISE *(with impatience).*
  Well? What is keeping you?
RAGUENEAU.   There! There you are!
    (Takes a third, and resigns himself to his fate.)
  The sonnet unto Phyllis! It is hard!
LISE.   I'm glad he has decided.
(Shrugging her shoulders.)   Nicodemus!
 *(Stands on a chair and sets about arranging dishes on
              a high sideboard.)*
RAGUENEAU *(taking advantage of the fact that she has
      turned her back, calls back the children, already
      at the door).*
  Pst, children! Give me back the lines to Phyllis
  And I will give six patties for your three.
  *(The children give the bag back to him, snatch the
  cakes, and run off. Ragueneau, smoothing out the
        paper, begins to declaim as he reads.)*
  "Phyllis!" On this sweet name a spot of butter—
  "Phyllis!"

              (Cyrano enters hurriedly.)

Scene III.

Ragueneau, Lise, Cyrano, afterwards the Musketeer.

CYRANO.   What time is it?
RAGUENEAU *(bowing to him ceremoniously).*
  Six.
CYRANO *(with emotion).*   In an hour!
            (Walks to and fro in the shop.)
RAGUENEAU *(following him).*

Bravo! I saw—

CYRANO. Well, what?

RAGUENEAU. Your fight!

CYRANO. Which one?

RAGUENEAU. At the Hôtel de Bourgogne!

CYRANO (*disdainfully*). Oh, the duel!

RAGUENEAU (*admiringly*).

The duel fought in verse!

LISE. He's full of it!

CYRANO. I'm glad to hear it.

RAGUENEAU (*fencing with a spit he has caught up*).
"*I shall thrust when I end the refrain!*"
Ah, how fine it was!
"*I shall thrust when I end the refrain.*"
(*With growing enthusiasm.*)
"*I shall thrust when I end*"—

CYRANO. What time is it?

RAGUENEAU (*stopping his fencing while he looks at the
clock*).
Five minutes after!—"*the refrain.*"
(*Straightens up.*) A ballade!
To think of writing one!

LISE (*to Cyrano who has absent-mindedly shaken her
hand as he passed her desk*).
You've hurt your hand?

CYRANO. Nothing. A little cut.

RAGUENEAU. You were in danger?

CYRANO. No, none at all.

LISE (*shaking her finger at him*). I think that you are lying!

CYRANO. And think you that would set my nose a-tremble?
'Twould have to be a most tremendous lie!
(*Changing his tone.*)
I wait for some one here. If not in vain,

    You will leave us alone.

RAGUENEAU.   But that I cannot.

    My poets soon will come—

LISE (*ironically*).   For their first meal.

CYRANO.   You'll get them hence when I shall give the
    signal.

    The time?

RAGUENEAU.   Ten minutes past.

CYRANO (*nervously sitting down at Ragueneau's table,
    and taking a sheet of paper*).

    A pen?

RAGUENEAU (*offering him the one at his ear*).

    A swan's quill!

A MUSKETEER (*with tremendous moustache, and speak-
    ing in stentorian tones, enters*).

    Greeting!

                (*Lise goes quickly to meet him.*)

CYRANO (*turning*).   Who's that?

RAGUENEAU.   A great friend of my wife's.

    A terrible warrior,—by what he says!

CYRANO (*taking the pen again and motioning to Rague-
    neau to withdraw*).

    Hush! Write,—seal—

(*aside*)   —give it to her—and escape.

                (*Throwing away the pen.*)

    Coward! May I be hanged if I have courage

    To speak to her a single word,—

(*To Ragueneau.*)   The time?

RAGUENEAU.   A quarter past.

CYRANO (*tapping his chest*).   Of those that I have here!

    While if I write—

(*Takes up the pen.*)   Oh! well, then! let us write it!

    The letter I have thought out to myself

A hundred times, so that it now is ready;
And if I put my soul beside the paper
I shall need only to recopy it.
(Writes. Behind the glass doors, thin and hesitating
figures are seen moving.)

Scene IV.

Ragueneau, Lise, the Musketeer. Cyrano, writing at a
little table. The Poets, dressed in black, with stockings slipping down and covered with mud.

LISE *(entering, to Ragueneau)*.
  Here are your scarecrows!
FIRST POET *(entering, to Ragueneau)*.   Colleague!
SECOND POET *(same action, shaking his hand.)*
  Honored colleague!
THIRD POET.   Eagle of pastry-cooks!
(sniffs)   It smells good here.
FOURTH POET. Phœbus of bakers!
FIFTH POET.   Apollo[2] of the oven!
RAGUENEAU *(surrounded, embraced, shaken by the hand)*.
  How speedily one feels at ease with them!
FIRST POET.   The crowd, collected at the Porte de Nesle,
  Delayed us.
SECOND POET.   Eight cut-purses, all a-bleeding
  With gaping sword-wounds, lay about the pavement!
CYRANO *(lifting his head a moment)*.
  Eight? It was seven, I thought.
                    (Returns to his letter.)
RAGUENEAU *(to Cyrano)*. Do you then know
  The hero of the battle?

CYRANO (*carelessly*).   I? No!

LISE (*to the Musketeer*).   And you?

THE MUSKETEER (*twisting his moustache*).
   Perhaps!

CYRANO (*still writing, is heard from time to time to mur-
       mur a word aside*).   I love you!

FIRST POET.   They say one man alone
   Put a whole band to rout!

SECOND POET.   A curious sight!
   The ground was strewn with cudgels and with pikes!

CYRANO (*writing*).   Your eyes—

THIRD POET.   To the Goldsmith's Quay the hats were
       strewn!

FIRST POET.   He must have been a savage one!

CYRANO (*same action*).   Your lips—

FIRST POET.   A giant terrible, who wrought these deeds!

CYRANO (*same action*).   And yet I faint with fear when
       I perceive you.

SECOND POET (*snatching a cake*).
   What verses have you written, Ragueneau, lately?

CYRANO (*same action.*)   Who love you—
(*Stops just as he is about to sign the letter, and gets up,
               putting it in his doublet.*)
   Signing's needless, I shall give it
   To her myself.

RAGUENEAU (*to the Second Poet*).   A recipe in verse.

THIRD POET (*taking his place near a platter of puffs*).
   Give us the poem!

FOURTH POET (*looking at a cake he has taken*).
   This cake has put on
   Its cap wrong-side before.
               (*Bites off the top.*)

FIRST POET.   This spice cake follows

The starveling rhymester, with its almond eyes,
And candy eyebrows!
> *(Takes the piece of spice-cake.)*

SECOND POET.   We are listening.

THIRD POET *(squeezing a cream-puff softly between his fingers).*

This cream puff's running over. It is laughing.

SECOND POET *(biting at the great lyre of pastry itself).*

For the first time the Lyre gives me food!

RAGUENEAU *(after getting ready to recite, coughing, settling his cap, and striking an attitude).*

A recipe in verse—

SECOND POET *(to the first, nudging him).*
Breakfast?

FIRST POET *(to the second).*   No, dinner!

RAGUENEAU.   *How to make almond cream tarts:*

> Beat some eggs till they be light,
> And frothy quite;
> Then, when light enough they seem,
> From a lemon squeeze the juice
> For your use,
> Then mix in sweet almond cream.
>
> Next with puff-paste, light as air,
> With great care
> Line your moulds up to the top;
> With skilled fingers shape the paste
> To your taste,
> Pour the cream in drop by drop.
>
> When filled with this frothy mass,
> Let them pass
> To the oven, till they seem

Brown enough, and you will see
Merrily
Emerge the tarts of almond cream.

THE POETS *(their mouths full)*.
   Charming! Delicious!
A POET *(choking)*.   Humph!
      (They retire into the background, still eating.)
CYRANO *(who has been watching them, goes towards
      Ragueneau)*.
   Soothed by your voice,
   Do you not see the way they stuff themselves?
RAGUENEAU *(smiling and in a lower voice)*.
   I see—but do not look, lest it should pain them;
   And, so to speak, my verses give to me
   A double pleasure, since I satisfy
   An amiable weakness of my own,
   The while I feed those who might hungry go!
CYRANO *(tapping him on the shoulder)*.
   I like you.
*(Ragueneau rejoins his friends, Cyrano follows him
      with his eyes, and then speaking rather sharply)*.
   Lise, come here!
LISE *(in tender discourse with the Musketeer, gives a
      start, and comes towards Cyrano)*.
   This warrior bold
   Besieges you?
LISE *(offended)*.   My eyes, with haughty glance,
   Know how to conquer any lover rash
   Who would assail my virtue.
CYRANO.   Eugh! your eyes,
   For conquerors, seem of a yielding spirit.
LISE *(choking)*.   But—

CYRANO (*raising his voice so that the Musketeer may
     hear him*).   To the wise a word—
          (*Bows to the Musketeer, and takes a post of
     observation at the door in the background, after
               having looked at the clock.*)
LISE (*to the Musketeer, who has merely returned Cyrano's
     bow*).   I wonder at you!
     Answer him—on his nose—
THE MUSKETEER.   On his nose, no!
          (*Withdraws quickly, Lise follows him.*)
CYRANO (*from the door in the background, motioning to
     Ragueneau to get the poets out of the way*).
     Pst!—
RAGUENEAU (*showing the poets the door on the right*).
     We shall find it better—
CYRANO (*growing impatient*).   Pst!—
RAGUENEAU (*pulling them along*).   To read Poetry—
FIRST POET (*in despair, with his mouth full*).   But the
     cakes!
SECOND POET.   Take them along.
     (*They all follow Ragueneau out in a procession, after
          making a clean sweep of all the cakes.*)

Scene V.

Cyrano, Roxane, the Duenna.

CYRANO.   I'll use the letter if I think there be
     The smallest hope—
(*Roxane appears behind the glass door, masked and fol-
     lowed by the duenna. Cyrano opens the door
     quickly.*)   Come in!
(*Walking up to the duenna.*)   A word with you!

THE DUENNA.   Two.

CYRANO.   Are you fond of sweets?

THE DUENNA.   To make me sick.

CYRANO (*quickly taking some of the paper bags from the counter*).

Here are two sonnets Benserade[3] has written—

THE DUENNA.   Pooh!

CYRANO.   Which I'll fill with wine-cakes.

THE DUENNA (*changing her expression*).

Oh!

CYRANO.   You like

These cream puffs also?

THE DUENNA.   Oh, I dote upon them!

CYRANO.   Six of them I will put within the bosom
Of a poem by Saint-Amant![4]   In these verses
Of Chapelain,[5] I'll put a piece of sponge cake,—
You like fresh cakes, then?

THE DUENNA.   Oh! I love them madly!

CYRANO (*filling her arms with the bags of cakes*).

Be kind enough to eat all these outside.

THE DUENNA.   But—

CYRANO (*pushing her out*).   Come not back till you
have finished them!

(*Closes the door, comes back to Roxane, and stops,
uncovered, at a respectful distance.*)

Scene VI.

Cyrano, Roxane; for a moment, the Duenna.

CYRANO.   Now let this moment be most blest of all
When, ceasing to forget I humbly breathe,
You come to say to me—to say to me—

ROXANE *(after having unmasked)*.
    To thank you first, because the knavish dolt
    Whom you put to the laugh, with your good sword,
    Is he whom a great lord—in love with me—
CYRANO.   De Guiche!
ROXANE *(lowering her eyes)*   —has tried to give me—
    for a husband.
CYRANO.   So-called?
(Bowing.) Then I have fought, and better so,
    For your bright eyes, not for my ugly nose.
ROXANE.   And then—I wished—but to make this avowal
    I needs must see in you the—almost brother,
    With whom I played, in the park, by the lake!
CYRANO.   Yes; you came every year to Bergerac.
ROXANE.   The reeds then furnished you with wood for
    swords.
CYRANO.   And the corn, yellow hair to deck your dolls.
ROXANE.   Those were the days of games—
CYRANO.   —of berry-picking.
ROXANE.   The days when you did all things that I wished!
CYRANO.   Roxane, in dresses short, was called Madeleine.
ROXANE.   And I was pretty then?
CYRANO.   You were not ugly.
ROXANE.   Sometimes, when you had cut your hand in
    climbing
    You ran to me; then I would play the mother,
    And say with voice that tried hard to be stern
                    (takes his hand),
    "What is this scratch now?"
(Stops in amazement.) Ah, too bad! And this?
            (Cyrano tries to draw back his hand.)
    No! Show it to me! What? At your age, still?
    How came it?

CYRANO.   Playing, at the Porte de Nesle.

ROXANE (*sitting at a table and dipping her handkerchief
    in a glass of water*).   Come!

CYRANO (*also sitting down*).   Like a fond and happy little mother!

ROXANE.   And tell me, while I wipe away the blood,
    How many were there?

CYRANO.   Oh! Not quite a hundred.

ROXANE.   Tell me!

CYRANO.   No, let it go! But you tell me
    That which just now you dared not—

ROXANE (*without letting go of his hand*).
    Now I dare.
    The past's sweet odor gives me courage new.
    Yes, now I dare. Listen, I love someone.

CYRANO.   Ah!

ROXANE.   Who has not guessed it!

CYRANO.   Ah!

ROXANE.   At least, not yet.

CYRANO.   Ah!

ROXANE.   But who soon will know, if he knows it not.

CYRANO.   Ah!

ROXANE.   A poor lad, who has loved me until now
    Timidly, from afar, nor dared to speak.

CYRANO.   Ah!

ROXANE.   Leave me your hand, it is all feverish!—
    But I have seen love trembling on his lips.

CYRANO.   Ah!

ROXANE (*finishing a little bandage for him made of her
    handkerchief*).
    And do you know, my cousin, that in fact
    He now is serving in your regiment!

CYRANO.   Ah!

ROXANE (*smiling*).   In your own company he's a cadet!

CYRANO.   Ah!

ROXANE.   His forehead shows his genius and his wit,
    He's young, proud, noble, brave, and fair—

CYRANO (*getting up, very pale*).   What, fair?

ROXANE.   Why, what's the matter?

CYRANO.   Nothing—'tis—
(*with a smile, showing his hand*)   — this wound.

ROXANE.   In fine, I love him. I must tell you, too,
    That I have seen him only at the play—

CYRANO.   You have not spoken?

ROXANE.   Only with our eyes.

CYRANO.   How do you know him then?

ROXANE.   Under the lindens,
    In the Place Royale, there is talk; and gossip
    Has told me—

CYRANO.   He is a cadet?

ROXANE.   He is.
    He's in the Guards.

CYRANO.   His name?

ROXANE.   The Baron Christian
    De Neuvillette—

CYRANO.   What? He's not in the Guards.

ROXANE.   Yes, since this morning, under Captain Car-
    bon
    De Castel-Jaloux.

CYRANO.   Ah! how quick is love!
    But my poor child—

THE DUENNA (*opening the door in the background*).
    Monsieur de Bergerac,
    I've finished all the cakes.

CYRANO.   Well, read the verses
    Upon the bags.   (*The duenna disappears.*)

My poor child, you who love
Keen wit and courtly speech, if he should be
A man unlearned, unpolished, in the rough!

ROXANE. No, he has hair like one of d'Urfê's heroes!

CYRANO.   His speech may lack the grace his hair displays!

ROXANE.   No, every word he speaks I know is brilliant.

CYRANO.   Yes, words are brilliant from a fair moustache;
But if he were a dolt!—

ROXANE (*tapping with her foot*).   Then I should die!

CYRANO (*after a pause*).
So you have brought me here to tell me that.
I cannot see the good of it, Madame!

ROXANE.   Ah! yesterday I had a deadly shock,—
I heard that you are Gascons, every one,
All of your company—

CYRANO.   And that we pick
Quarrels with all recruits, who by mere favor
Gain entrance to our ranks of Gascon blood,
And are not Gascons? That is what you heard?

ROXANE.   Think how I trembled for him!

CYRANO (*between his teeth*).   With good reason!

ROXANE.   But yesterday when you appeared to us
So mighty and so brave, holding your own
Against the rabble, punishing that knave,
I thought—if he but would, whom all men fear—

CYRANO.   'Tis well, I will protect your little baron.

ROXANE.   Ah, then you will protect him well for me?
I've always had so warm a friendship for you!

CYRANO.   Yes, yes.

ROXANE.   You'll be his friend?

CYRANO.   I'll be his friend.

ROXANE.   And he shall fight no duels?

CYRANO. On my oath!
ROXANE. I am so fond of you! Now I must go.
  (*Quickly puts on her mask, and a bit of lace over her
          head, and absent-mindedly.*)
  But you have not yet told me of the battle
  Last night. It must have been a mighty feat—
  Tell him to write.
        (*Throws him a little kiss with her fingers.*)
  I am so fond of you!
CYRANO. Yes, yes.
ROXANE. Five score against you? Well, good-bye,
  We are great friends?
CYRANO. Yes, yes.
ROXANE. Tell him to write.
  A hundred!   You will tell me later. Now
  I cannot stay. A hundred! Oh! what courage!
CYRANO (*bowing to her*).   I have done better since.
  (*Exit Roxane. Cyrano remains motionless, his eyes
  fixed on the ground. Silence for a time. The door on
  the right opens and Ragueneau's head appears.*)

Scene VII.

Cyrano, Ragueneau, the Poets, Carbon de Castel-
  Jaloux, the Cadets, the Crowd, etc., afterwards De
  Guiche.

RAGUENEAU.   May we come back?
CYRANO (*without moving*).   Yes.
  (*Ragueneau gives the signal and his friends come
  back. At the same time, at the door in the background,
  Carbon de Castel-Jaloux appears, in his uniform*)

> as Captain of the Guards, making sweeping
>   gestures as he perceives Cyrano.)

CARBON DE CASTEL-JALOUX.   There he is now!

CYRANO (*raising his head*).   Captain!

CARBON (*in exultation*).   Our hero!
  We know the story! Thirty of my men
  Are waiting—

CYRANO (*drawing back*).   But—

CARBON (*trying to draw him along*). Come now! They
    wish to see you.

CYRANO.   No!

CARBON.   They're drinking at the tavern opposite.

CYRANO.   I—

CARBON (*going back to the door, and calling behind the
            scenes in a thundering voice*).
  He refuses. He's in an ill humor!

A VOICE (*without*).   Ah, by the Lord!

(*A tumult without, noise of swords and spurs approaching.*)

CARBON.   You hear them cross the street!
    (*The Cadets enter the cook-shop with a chorus of
            Gascon oaths and exclamations.*)

RAGUENEAU (*drawing back in alarm*).
  Gentlemen, are you all from Gascony?

THE CADETS.   All!

A CADET (*to Cyrano*).   Bravo!

CYRANO.   Baron!

ANOTHER (*shaking his hands*).   Hurrah!

CYRANO.   Baron!

THIRD CADET (*embracing him*).   Greeting!

CYRANO.   Baron!

SEVERAL CADETS.   Embrace him!

CYRANO (*not knowing whom to answer*).
  Baron! baron! spare me!

RAGUENEAU. Gentlemen, is each one of you a baron?

THE CADETS. All!

RAGUENEAU. Are they?

FIRST CADET. Just our crests would build a tower!

LE BRET (*entering and running towards Cyrano*).
 A crowd, led by your escort of last night,
 Is looking for you madly everywhere!

CYRANO (*in alarm*).
 You did not tell them where I am?

LE BRET (*rubbing his hands*). I did!

A TRADESMAN (*entering, followed by a crowd*).
 Monsieur, the whole Marais[6] is coming hither!
 (*The street outside is full of people. Carriages and
    sedan chairs block the way.*)

LE BRET (*aside, with a smile, to Cyrano*).
 And Roxane?

CYRANO (*brusquely*). Hush!

THE CROWD (*shouting without*). Cyrano!
 (*A mob bursts into the cook-shop. Confusion and
    shouting.*)

RAGUENEAU (*standing on a table*). In they swarm!
 They're breaking everything! 'Tis glorious!

PEOPLE (*surrounding Cyrano*).
 My friend! My friend!

CYRANO. I had not yesterday
 So many friends!

LE BRET (*delighted*). Success!

A LITTLE MARQUIS (*running up with outstretched hands*).
 If thou didst know—

CYRANO. If thou?—if thou?— Now what have we in
 common?

ANOTHER MARQUIS. Monsieur, may I present you to
 some ladies

Who are waiting in my carriage?

CYRANO (*coldly*).   Who will first
Present you to me.

LE BRET (*in amazement*).   What's the matter?

CYRANO.   Hush!

A MAN OF LETTERS (*with a writing-case*).
May I have the details?—

CYRANO.   No!

LE BRET (*nudging him*).   The inventor
Of the "Gazette"—Théophraste Renaudot![7]

CYRANO.   No matter!

LE BRET.   'Tis the sheet that tells so much.
They say this new idea has a great future.

A POET (*coming forward*).   Monsieur—

CYRANO.   Another!

THE POET.   I should like to make
A pentacrostic[8] on your name—

A MAN (*also advancing*).   Monsieur—

CYRANO.   Enough!
(*A movement in the crowd. People take their places.
De Guiche appears, escorted by officers. Enter Cuigy,
Brissaille, and the other officers who started with
Cyrano at the end of the First Act. Cuigy approaches
Cyrano rapidly.*)

CUIGY (*to Cyrano*).   Monsieur De Guiche!
(*Murmuring. All take position.*)   He represents
Marshal de Gassion!

DE GUICHE (*bowing to Cyrano*).   Who sends to you
His compliments upon your latest feat,
The news of which has reached him.

THE CROWD.   Bravo! Bravo!

CYRANO (*with a bow*).   The Marshal is expert in daring
deeds.

DE GUICHE.   He would have disbelieved, save on the
     oath
   Of these who saw it.
CUIGY.   With our very eyes!
LE BRET (*aside, to Cyrano, who seems absent-minded*).
     But—
CYRANO.   Hush!
LE BRET.   You seem in pain!
CYRANO (*with a start, and quickly drawing himself up*).
     Before this crowd?
(*His moustache bristles; he throws out his chest.*)   I
     seem in pain?— You'll see!
DE GUICHE (*to whom Cuigy has been whispering*).
   Your life already
   Is full of doughty deeds. With these mad Gascons
   You're serving, are you not?
CYRANO.   With the Cadets.
A CADET (*with stentorian voice*).   With us!
DE GUICHE (*looking at the Gascons, standing in line be-
     hind Cyrano*).   Ah! Ah! All these, of lordly mien,
   Are then the famous—
CARBON DE CASTEL-JALOUX.   Cyrano!
CYRANO.   What, Captain?
CARBON.   Since now my company has filled its roster,
   Present it to the Count in all due form.
CYRANO (*advancing two paces towards De Guiche and
     indicating the Cadets*).

     These be cadets of Gascony,
     Carbon de Castel-Jaloux's men:
     They fight, they lie full shamelessly,
     These be cadets of Gascony!
     Their talk is all of heraldry—

Nobler are they than highwaymen;
These be cadets of Gascony,
Carbon de Castel-Jaloux's men.

With stork's long leg and eagle's eye,
And cat's moustache and wolf's keen fangs,
Thrusting the growling rabble by,
With stork's long leg and eagle's eye,
They march, hats cocked on heads held high,—
The holes hid, where the feather hangs,—
With stork's long leg and eagle's eye,
And cat's moustache and wolf's keen fangs!

Friends Belly-thrust and Break-your-pate,
Such are their nicknames soft and sweet;
On glory they're intoxicate!
Friends Belly-thrust and Break-your-pate.
Where quarrels start at fastest rate,
These are the places where they meet.
Friends Belly-thrust and Break-your-pate.
Such are their nicknames soft and sweet!

See the cadets of Gascony,
Who plant horns on the husband's brow!
Oh, woman, loved so tenderly,
See the cadets of Gascony!
Let husbands old frown angrily,
Let cuckoos sing from every bough!
See the cadets of Gascony,
Who plant horns on the husband's brow!

DE GUICHE (*carelessly seated in an armchair which
    Ragueneau has quickly brought him*).
  A poet is a modern luxury,
  Will you belong to me?

CYRANO.   No, sir, to no one.

DE GUICHE.   Your dash amused my uncle Richelieu
Yesterday. I would help you with him.

LE BRET (*dazzled*).   Lord!

DE GUICHE.   I take it you have done a play in verse!

LE BRET (*whispering to Cyrano*).
You'll get your "Agrippina"[9] played, my friend.

DE GUICHE.   Take it to him.

CYRANO (*tempted and rather pleased*). Well—

DE GUICHE.   He is most expert.
He'll only change a line or two of yours!

CYRANO (*whose face has immediately flushed*).
Impossible, Monsieur; my blood runs cold,
To think of changing even one small comma.

DE GUICHE.   But when he likes a verse, my friend, he
pays,
And pays right dear.

CYRANO.   He pays for it less dear
Than I do, when I've made a verse I like;
I pay for it, singing it to myself.

DE GUICHE.   You're proud.

CYRANO.   Ah! really, you have noticed it?

A CADET (*entering with a collection of shabby hats spit-
ted on his sword, their plumes bedraggled and
holes through the brims*).
Look, Cyrano! this morning on the quay,
What strangely feathered game we gathered in;
The hats left in the rout—

CARBON.   The spoils of war!

EVERY ONE (*laughing*).   Ha! ha!

CUIGY.   Whoever set this band of cutthroats
Is in a rage to-day.

BRISSAILLE.   Is it known who?

DE GUICHE. 'Twas I! (*The laughter ceases.*)
    I charged them to chastise—a task
    One does not do one's self—a drunken rhymester.
              (*A constrained silence.*)

THE CADET (*in an undertone to Cyrano, showing him the hats*).
    What shall we make of them? A stew? They're greasy.

CYRANO (*taking the sword upon which they are impaled, salutes, and lets them all slip off at De Guiche's feet*).
    Monsieur, will you return them to your friends?

DE GUICHE (*rising, in a peremptory tone*).
    My bearers and my chair, at once,—I go.
              (*To Cyrano angrily.*)
    You, sir!—

A VOICE (*in the street, shouting*).
    The bearers of my lord the Comte
    De Guiche!

DE GUICHE (*regaining his self-control, with a smile*).
    Have you read "Don Quixote"?

CYRANO. Yes,
    And 'neath this crack-brain's name I find myself.

DE GUICHE. Bethink yourself upon—

A BEARER (*appearing in the background*).
    The chair is here.

DE GUICHE. The chapter of the windmills![10]

CYRANO (*bowing*). The thirteenth.

DE GUICHE. When one attacks them, it will oft be-
    fall—

CYRANO. Then I attack folk turned by every wind?

DE GUICHE. That while their sails in circles sweep
    about

They'll land you in the mud!

CYRANO.   Or in the stars!

(Exit De Guiche. He is seen getting into his chair. The gentlemen of his escort withdraw whispering together. Le Bret accompanies them to the door. The crowd departs.)

Scene VIII.

Cyrano, Le Bret, the Cadets, the latter seated at Tables
  to the Right and Left, and being served with Food
  and Drink.

CYRANO *(bowing to them mockingly as they go out with-
      out daring to bow to him).*

  Gentlemen! Gentlemen—

LE BRET *(returning in despair, throwing up his arms).*

  What a misfortune!

CYRANO.   Oh, you! you'll scold!

LE BRET.   You surely must admit

  Murdering every passing chance becomes

  Exaggerated.

CYRANO.   Well, I exaggerate.

LE BRET *(in triumph).*   Ah!

CYRANO.   But upon principle, and as a practice,

  I find it well thus to exaggerate.

LE BRET.   If you would lay aside your guardsman's
      spirit,

  Fortune and glory—

CYRANO.   And what must I do?

  Seek some protector strong, get me a patron

  And like some humble vine, that twines a trunk,

  Upheld by it, the while it strips its bark,

Climb by mere artifice, not rise by strength?
No, thank you. Dedicate, as others do,
Verses to bankers? Make myself a clown
In hopes of seeing on a statesman's lips
A friendly smile appear? I thank you, no!
Shall I be a toad-eater all my days?
My waist worn out by bending, and my skin
Grown quickly soiled in the region of my knees?
Or shall I show how limber is my back?—
No, thank you! On both shoulders carry water,
And sit the fence a-straddle, while I flatter
Each to his face, and feather my own nest?
No, thank you! Raise myself from step to step,
Become the little great man of a clique,
And steer my boat, with madrigals for oars,
And sighs of ancient dames to fill my sails?
No, thank you! Pay the editor De Sercy,
For publishing my poems? No, I thank you!
Or shall I have myself proclaimed as pope
By councils held in drinking-shops by fools?
No, thank you! Shall I make a reputation
Upon one sonnet, rather than write others?
Find talent only in the commonplace?
Be constantly in fear of errant sheets,
And always say: "Oh, let my name be seen
Upon the pages of the 'Mercure François'?"
No, thank you! Plan, be pale, and be afraid,
And make a call rather than write a poem,
Prepare petitions, have myself presented?
No, thank you! No, I thank you! No! But—sing,
Dream, laugh, and go about, alone and free,
Have eyes that see things clear, and voice that rings,
And, if you like, wear your hat wrong side front;

Fight for a yes or no—or make a poem;
Work without thought of fortune or of glory;
Fly to the moon in fancy, if you wish!
Write not a word that comes not from your heart,
And still be modest; tell yourself, "My child,
Content yourself with flowers and fruits,—with
    leaves,—
If you have gathered them in your own garden!"
Then, if by chance you gain some small success,
No tribute money need you pay to Cæsar,
And all the honor is your very own.
In short, scorning to be the clinging vine,
When you are neither oak nor linden tree,
Mount not so high perhaps, but all alone!

LE BRET.   Alone, so be it! But not one against all!
How did you get this mad idea of yours
Of making enemies where'er you go?

CYRANO.   From seeing you making so many friends,
And smiling at these crowds of friends you make
With lips pursed up and wrinkled! I prefer
To have few bows to make when I go forth,
And gladly shout, "Another enemy!"

LE BRET.   But this is madness!

CYRANO.   Well, yes, 'tis my weakness.
To displease is my pleasure. Hate I love.
My friend, if you but knew how light one walks
Under the fusillade[11] of hostile eyes;
What pleasant little spots upon one's doublet
Are made by envy's gall and cowards' spittle!—
But the soft friendship you wrap round yourself
Is like those great Italian collars, floating,
And made of openwork, in which your neck
Grows soft like to a woman's: wearing them

One feels at ease—but holds his head less high;
For, having neither order nor support,
It weakly rolls about on every side.
While, as for me, Hate sheathes me every day,
Gives me a ruff that holds my head erect.
Every new enemy is another pleat,
A new constraint, and one more ray of glory,
For, like in all points to the Spanish ruff,
Hate is at once a collar and a halo!

LE BRET (*after a pause, putting his arm through Cyrano's*).
Be proud and bitter to the world, but softly
Tell me quite simply that she loves thee not.

CYRANO (*sharply*).   Hush!

(*After a moment Christian enters and joins the Cadets.
They do not speak to him; at last he sits down at a
small table, where Lise waits on him.*

Scene IX.

Cyrano, Le Bret, the Cadets, Christian de Neuvillette.

A CADET (*seated at a table in the background, glass in
hand*).   Cyrano!
(*Cyrano turns.*)   The story?
CYRANO.   In a moment.
(*Withdraws on Le Bret's arm. They talk in undertones.*)
THE CADET (*rising and coming forward*).
The story of the fight! 'Twill be a lesson—
(*stops before the table where Christian is seated*)
—For this untried recruit.
CHRISTIAN (*raising his head*).   Untried recruit?
ANOTHER CADET.   Yes, northern weakling!

CHRISTIAN. Weakling, did you say?

FIRST CADET (*mockingly*).
  Monsieur de Neuvillette, learn this one thing:
  There is one object which we do not mention
  More than the rope in the household of one hanged.

CHRISTIAN. And what is that?

ANOTHER CADET (*in an impressive voice*).
  Behold me!
(*Mysteriously touches his finger to his nose three times.*)
  Understand?

CHRISTIAN. Ah! 'tis the—

ANOTHER. Hush—that word is never uttered!
  (*Indicates Cyrano, who is talking with Le Bret in the
      background.*)
  Or 'tis with him there you will have to do.

ANOTHER (*who has silently sat down on the table behind
    him, while he has been turning to face the others*).
  Two men he slew because he liked it not
  That they talked through their noses.

ANOTHER (*rising from under the table where he has
    crawled on all fours, in a hollow voice*).
  And one cannot
  Without departing, cut off in his youth,
  Make one allusion to the fatal feature!

ANOTHER (*laying his hand on his shoulder*).
  One word's enough! I said a word?—a gesture!
  To draw one's kerchief is to draw one's shroud.
(*Silence. All around him fold their arms and watch him.
  He rises and walks towards Carbon de Castel-Jaloux,
who is talking with an officer and seems to see nothing.*)

CHRISTIAN. Captain!

CARBON (*turning and looking him over*).
  Monsieur?

CHRISTIAN.   What is the thing to do,
   When Southrons are too boastful?
CARBON.   Prove to them
   One can be from the North, and brave.
                    (Turns his back on him.)
CHRISTIAN.   I thank you.
FIRST CADET *(to Cyrano).*   Your story now!
ALL.   His story!
CYRANO *(coming forward towards them).*
   What, my story?
   *(All draw their benches towards him, and form a
   group, craning their necks. Christian straddles a
                   chair.)*
   Well: I was marching all alone, to meet them,
   The moon shone in the sky like a great watch,
   When some watchmaker, suddenly, with care,
   Starting to draw a piece of cloudy cotton
   Across the silver case of this round watch,
   The night became the blackest ever seen;
   And as there are no lights upon the quays,
   Good Lord! you could not see beyond—
CHRISTIAN.   Your nose?
   *(Silence. Every one rises slowly. They look at Cyrano
     in terror. He breaks off in amazement. A pause.)*
CYRANO.   Who is that man there?
A CADET *(in an undertone).*   He's a man who came
   This morning.
CYRANO *(taking a step towards Christian).*
   Did you say this morning?
CARBON *(in an undertone).*   Named Baron de Neuvil—
CYRANO *(quickly stopping).*   Ah, 'tis well—
*(Turns pale, then red, and makes another movement as
    if to fling himself upon Christian.)*   I—

(Then regains his composure and says in a quiet voice.)
    Well—

                        (Begins again.)
    As I was saying—
(With a burst of anger in his voice.)   God—
(Continues in a natural tone.)   —you could not see.
    (Amazement. They take their seats, watching him.)
    And so I went, thinking that for a beggar
    I was about to offend some mighty prince,
    Who surely would bear me a bitter grudge;
    In short, that rashly and without concern,
    I was about to thrust—
CHRISTIAN.   Your nose?
CYRANO.   —my fingers
    Between the bark and tree, since this great man
    Might well be strong enough to deal a blow
    Upon—
CHRISTIAN.   Your nose?
CYRANO *(wiping the sweat from his face).*
    —upon my meddling fingers.
    But then I added: "Gascon, do your duty!
    Cyrano, march!" Then, onward in the dark,
    I go and feel—
CHRISTIAN.   A fillip on the nose?
CYRANO.   I parry. Suddenly I find myself—
CHRISTIAN.   Nose against nose—
CYRANO *(leaping at him).*   Damnation!
    *(All the Gascons rush forward to see; when Cyrano
      reaches Christian he regains his self-control and
                        continues.)*
    With a hundred
    Roistering ruffians, stinking—
CHRISTIAN.   'Neath your nose—

CYRANO (*pale and smiling*).
   —With sour wine and onions! Then I rush
   Head down—
CHRISTIAN.   Nose on the scent—
CYRANO.   And so I charge:
   Two I rip up! I run another through!
   The some one lunges—Paf! I answer—
CHRISTIAN.   Pif!
CYRANO (*exploding*).
   The devil! Out with you!
      (*All the Cadets rush towards the doors.*)
FIRST CADET.   The tiger wakes!
CYRANO.   Every one! With this man leave me alone!
SECOND CADET.   We'll find him cut in mincemeat!
RAGUENEAU.   What, in mincemeat?
ANOTHER CADET.   Filling one of your patties!
RAGUENEAU.   I grow pale
   And limp as any napkin.
CARBON.   Let us go!
ANOTHER.   He will not leave a single morsel of him!
ANOTHER.   I die of fright thinking what will befall!
ANOTHER (*closing the door on the right*).   Something
   most terrible!
(*They all go out, some by the rear, some by the sides,
some by the stairway. Cyrano and Christian remain
face to face, and look at each other for a moment.*)

Scene X.

Cyrano, Christian.

CYRANO.   Give me your hand!
CHRISTIAN.   Monsieur—

CYRANO.   Brave man!

CHRISTIAN.   But—

CYRANO.   Very brave; I like it!

CHRISTIAN.   But tell me?—

CYRANO.   Come, your hand, I am her brother.

CHRISTIAN.   Whose?

CYRANO.   Hers!

CHRISTIAN.   What?

CYRANO.   Roxane's!

CHRISTIAN (*rushing to him*).   Heavens! You? Her brother?

CYRANO.   Yes; or almost: a cousin like a brother.

CHRISTIAN.   She's told you?—

CYRANO.   All!

CHRISTIAN.   She loves me?

CYRANO.   That may be.

CHRISTIAN (*taking his hand*).

   Monsieur, I am so happy to have met you!

CYRANO.   This is what might be called a sudden friendship.

CHRISTIAN.   Forgive me—

CYRANO (*looking at him and laying his hand on his shoulder*).   True, he is a handsome rascal!

CHRISTIAN.   If you knew, sir, how I admire you.

CYRANO.   But all these "noses" which—

CHRISTIAN.   I take them back.

CYRANO.   Roxane to-night expects a letter—

CHRISTIAN.   Ah!

CYRANO.   What?

CHRISTIAN.   I shall spoil my chances if I speak!

CYRANO.   Why?

CHRISTIAN.   I'm so stupid that I die of shame!

CYRANO.   No, you are not, since you take count of it,

And your attack on me was not so stupid.

CHRISTIAN.   Bah! Words come quickly when one starts
   to fight.
Yes, I may have a ready soldier's wit,
But before women I must hold my tongue.
Their eyes smile kindly on me as I pass—

CYRANO.   And when you stop, do not their hearts the like?

CHRISTIAN.   No; for I am—I know it, and I tremble—
A man who cannot talk of love.

CYRANO.   I think,
Had I been one fashioned more carefully
I could have talked of it among the best.

CHRISTIAN.   Oh, for the power to speak one's thoughts
   with grace!

CYRANO.   To walk about, a handsome musketeer!

CHRISTIAN.   Roxane is learnèd, I shall surely kill
All her illusions!

CYRANO.   If I only had
Such an interpreter to speak my soul!

CHRISTIAN (*in despair*).
I need fair words.

CYRANO (*abruptly*).   And I will lend them to you!
And you lend me your conquering comeliness;
And so combined together let us make
A hero of romance!

CHRISTIAN.   What?

CYRANO.   You could learn
To speak the words I'll teach you—

CHRISTIAN.   You suggest?—

CYRANO.   Roxane shall never lose her fond illusions!
Together let us win her, say you so?
And shall I breathe in you my very soul,
From my buff jerkin to your broidered doublet?—

CHRISTIAN.   But, Cyrano!—

CYRANO.   You will?

CHRISTIAN.   You frighten me!

CYRANO. You fear lest by yourself you chill her heart?
  Shall we not join your lips and my fine words?
  And very soon you'll fold her in your arms.

CHRISTIAN. Your eyes are gleaming!

CYRANO.   Will you?

CHRISTIAN.   What! Will that
  Give you such pleasure?

CYRANO *(with elation).*   That—
  (stopping himself, and in the tone of an artist pleased
              with his work)
  —that will amuse me.
  'Tis an experiment to tempt a poet.
  Shall we be each the other's complement?
  I shall walk in the shadow by your side,
  You will be my good looks and I your wit.

CHRISTIAN.   But I can never write the needed letter
  Which must be sent forthwith—

CYRANO *(taking from his doublet the letter he had writ-*
     ten.)   There is your letter!

CHRISTIAN.   What?

CYRANO.   There is nothing lacking but the name.

CHRISTIAN.   I—

CYRANO.   You can send it. Reassure yourself.
  It is a good one.

CHRISTIAN.   You—

CYRANO.   We always have them
  With us: letters to Chloris[12]—in our minds;
  For we are such as have for sweethearts only
  Dreams breathed into the bubble of a name.
  Take it, and change these fancies into facts,—

I shot at random these pleas, these avowals,—
And all these flitting birds you'll bring to perch!
You'll see that in this letter I was—take it!—
As eloquent as I was insincere!
Take it, and end the talk!

CHRISTIAN.   Will not some words
Need to be changed. Written thus at a venture,
Will it fit Roxane?

CYRANO.   'Twill fit her like a glove.

CHRISTIAN.   But—

CYRANO.   Self-conceit so well deceives itself,
Roxane will think 'twas written all for her!

CHRISTIAN.   My friend!

*(Throws himself into Cyrano's arms. They stand
embracing each other.)*

Scene XI.

Cyrano, Christian, the Gascons, the Musketeer, Lise.

A CADET *(partly opening the door)*.   No word. The si-
lence of the grave.
I dare not look—
(Puts his head in.)   What?

ALL THE CADETS *(entering and seeing Cyrano and
Christian embracing)*.
Ah! Oh!

A CADET.   What is this?
(General surprise.)

THE MUSKETEER *(mockingly)*.   Well?

CARBON.   Mild as a saint our demon has become?
Smitten upon one cheek he turns the other?

THE MUSKETEER.   Now you may speak to him about his
   nose.
             (Triumphantly calling Lise.)
   Oh! Lise. You'll see!
             (Pretending to be smelling the air.)
   Oh! Oh! It is surprising!
   This odor!
(Approaching Cyrano.)   Sir, have you not noticed it?
   What does it smell of here?
CYRANO *(boxing his ears).*   I think a nosegay!
*(Rejoicing. The Cadets find that Cyrano is unchanged.
             They turn somersaults.)*

CURTAIN.

THIRD ACT

Roxane's Kiss.

*A small square in the old Marais, with ancient houses,
   and a perspective of narrow streets. To the right,
   Roxane's house, and the wall of its garden, bordered
   with abundant foliage. Above the door, a window
   and balcony. A bench before the threshold. Vines
   climb the wall; jasmine wreathes the balcony and
   hangs quivering. By means of the bench and stones
   jutting out from the wall it is easy to climb to the balcony. Opposite, an old house of the same style, of
   brick and stone, with a door of entrance. The knocker
   of this door is wrapped with linen like an injured
   thumb. When the curtain rises the duenna is seated
   on the bench. The window is wide open on Roxane's
   balcony. Ragueneau, dressed in a sort of livery, is*

*standing by the duenna. He is finishing a narrative,
and wiping his eyes.*

Scene I.

Ragueneau, the Duenna; then Roxane, Cyrano, and two
Pages.

RAGUENEAU.   And then she left me for a musketeer!
   I was alone and ruined—I hanged myself,
   Monsieur de Bergerac came and cut me down,
   And offers me to his cousin as a steward.
THE DUENNA.   But how do you explain this plight of
      yours?
RAGUENEAU.   Lise loved the soldiers; I was fond of
      poets!
   And Mars ate all the cakes Apollo left;
   And so—you understand—the end soon came.
THE DUENNA (*rising and calling towards the open win-
      dow*).
   Roxane, they're waiting for us,—are you ready?
ROXANE.   I'm putting on my cloak.
THE DUENNA (*to Cyrano, pointing to the door opposite*)
   They wait for us
   Opposite, at Clomire's. In her retreat
   She keeps an exchange for wits. This afternoon
   There'll be a discourse on the Tender Passion.
RAGUENEAU.   The Tender Passion?
THE DUENNA (*simpering*).   Certainly.
(*Calling towards the window.*)   Roxane!
   You must come down, or we shall miss the discourse

Upon the Tender Passion!

ROXANE'S VOICE.   I am coming.

>   (*A sound of stringed instruments is heard*
>   *approaching.*)

CYRANO'S VOICE (*singing in the wings*).

La, la! la, la!

THE DUENNA (*surprised*).   They're playing a piece for us!

CYRANO (*followed by two Pages carrying lutes*).

That note's a demi-semi-quaver, fool!

FIRST PAGE (*ironically*).

You know what is a demi-semi-quaver?

CYRANO.   I'm a musician, like all Gassendi's pupils!

THE PAGE (*playing and singing*).   La, la!

CYRANO (*snatching away the lute and continuing the
    bar*).

I can go on—La, la! La, la!

ROXANE (*appearing on the balcony*).

'T is you.

CYRANO (*going on with the air, and singing*).

'T is I—come to salute your lilies,

And to pay my respects unto your roses!

ROXANE.   I'm coming down (*leaves the balcony*).

THE DUENNA (*indicating the Pages*).

Who are these *virtuosi?*

CYRANO. It is a bet I won from D'Assoucy.

We argued warmly on a point of grammar,

When suddenly he pointed to these giants

Who strike the strings with such a skilful hand,

And always form his escort; saying to me,

"I lay you a day of music"—and he lost!

And now, till Phœbus starts another round,

I have these lutists at my heels all day,

Musical witnesses of all I do.

At first 'twas charming, now I find it palls.
                    (To the musicians.)
Go—play a minuet to Montfleury.
        (The Pages start to go out. To the duenna.)
I came to ask Roxane, as every night—
            (To the Pages as they go out.)
Play on—and off the key!
(To the duenna.)   —Whether her friend
    Is still perfection?

ROXANE *(coming out of the house)*.
    Ah! how fair he is,
    And what a mind he has, and how I love him!

CYRANO *(smiling)*.
    Christian has such a mind?

ROXANE.   Yes, more than you!

CYRANO.   That I admit.

ROXANE.   I think there could not be
    A better framer of those pretty phrases
    Which may be naught, and yet are everything.
    Sometimes he seems distraught,—his Muse is gone;
    Then, all at once, he says such charming things!

CYRANO *(skeptically)*.   Really?

ROXANE.   This is too much. See what men are!
    Because a man has looks, he has no brains!

CYRANO.   Can he talk of the heart in clever fashion?

ROXANE.   He more than talks, he teaches!

CYRANO.   Does he write?

ROXANE. Yes, even better! Listen to a bit.
                    (Declaiming.)
    "The more you steal my heart, the more I have."
(Triumphantly to Cyrano.)   Well?

CYRANO.   Pooh!

ROXANE.   And this: *"But since I need another*

To suffer with, if you keep mine yourself,
Send me your own."

CYRANO.   Sometimes he has too much;
And sometimes not enough. What does he want?

ROXANE.   You grate on me! It is the jealousy—

CYRANO *(giving a start)*.   What!

ROXANE.   —of an author that quite eats you up!
And this, the very tenderest of them all:
"Believe me that my heart makes but one cry
To you; and that if kisses could be written,
Madame, you'd read my letter with your lips."

CYRANO *(smiling with satisfaction in spite of himself)*.
Ha, ha! those lines are,—eh, eh!
        (Stopping himself, and with disdain.)
—pretty weak!

ROXANE.   And this—

CYRANO *(delighted)*.   You know his letters, then, by
    heart?

ROXANE.   All!

CYRANO.   There's naught else to say; 'tis flattering!

ROXANE.   He is a master.

CYRANO *(modestly)*.   Oh!—a master!—

ROXANE *(peremptorily)*.   Yes!
A master.

CYRANO.   So be it then—a master!

THE DUENNA *(who had withdrawn, coming back
    quickly)*.   Monsieur de Guiche *(To Cyrano, push-
    ing him towards the house.)*
Go in—perhaps 'twere better
He should not find you here; because it might
Put him upon the scent—

ROXANE *(to Cyrano)*.   Of my dear secret!
He loves me; he has power; he must not know!

For he might deal my love a cruel stroke.
CYRANO (*going into the house*).
   "Well, very well!
   (*De Guiche appears.*)

Scene II.

Roxane, De Guiche; the Duenna, in the Background.

ROXANE (*to De Guiche, making him a courtesy*).   I'm
   going out.
DE GUICHE.   I come to take my leave.
ROXANE.   You go away?
DE GUICHE.   To the war!
ROXANE.   Ah?
DE GUICHE.   Yes, to-night.
ROXANE.   Ah!
DE GUICHE.   I am under orders. We besiege
   Arras—
ROXANE.   A siege?
DE GUICHE.   Yes, but my departure
   Seems to leave you indifferent.
ROXANE.   Oh!
DE GUICHE.   As for me,
   I'm in despair!   When shall we meet again?
   You know that I am to command the force?
ROXANE (*indifferently*).   Bravo!
DE GUICHE.   The regiment of the Guards—
ROXANE (*interested at once*).   The Guards?
DE GUICHE.   In which your cousin serves, that braggart
   bold;
   I shall have my revenge on him down there.

ROXANE (*choking with emotion*).   The Guards are going?
DE GUICHE (*smiling*).   'Tis my regiment.
ROXANE (*falling back on the bench, aside*).
    Christian!
DE GUICHE.   What is the matter?
ROXANE (*much moved*).   This—departure—
    Will break my heart! To care for any one
    And know him at the war!
DE GUICHE (*surprised and charmed*).   For the first time
    To speak me kindly, the day I go away!
ROXANE (*changing her tone, and fanning herself*).
    Then—you would take revenge upon my cousin?
DE GUICHE.   You're on his side?
ROXANE.   Oh, no! against!
DE GUICHE.   You see him?
ROXANE.   Seldom.
DE GUICHE.   One meets him everywhere with one
    Of the Cadets.
(*Trying to think of the name.*)   This Neuvillen—viller—
ROXANE.   A tall man?
DE GUICHE.   Blond.
ROXANE.   Flaxen-haired—
DE GUICHE.   Handsome!—
ROXANE.   Pooh!—
DE GUICHE.   But somewhat stupid.
ROXANE.   Yes, he seems to be!
                    (*Changing her tone.*)
    But your revenge on Cyrano—Perhaps
    'Tis to put him under fire, which he loves?—
    That were small comfort. As for me, I know
    The way to break his heart!
DE GUICHE.   And how is that?
ROXANE.   But let the regiment depart, and leave him,

With folded arms, in Paris, through the war,
With his beloved Cadets. That is the way
To rouse a man like him to bitter wrath,
'Twill punish him to keep him out of danger.

DE GUICHE. A woman's wit!—and no one but a woman
Would think of such a trick!

ROXANE.   He'll eat his heart out;
His friends will gnaw their fists, thus left behind;
And you will be revenged.

DE GUICHE (*drawing nearer*).   You love me then
A little?

(*She smiles.*)   In thus taking up my grudge
I fain would see a proof of love, Roxane!

ROXANE.   A proof of love it is.

DE GUICHE (*showing several sealed packets*).
Here are the orders,
Which will be sent this moment to each troop,
Except—

(*detaches one*)—this one, for the Cadets.
(*Puts it in his pocket.*)   I keep it!
                    (*Smiling.*)
Ah! Ah! Ah! Cyrano!—his thirst for battle!
You play these tricks on people then?

ROXANE.   Sometimes.

DE GUICHE (*very close to her*).
You fill me with delight! Listen: to-night
I should begone—but —go, when you are moved?
Listen: hard by, in the Rue d'Orléans,
There stands a convent, founded by the head
Of the Capuchins'—Father Athanasius.
A layman cannot enter; but the fathers
May stretch a point for me; their sleeves are large,
They'll cover me with ease. These are the monks

Who wait on Richelieu[2] in his own household;
Dreading the uncle, they will fear the nephew.
People will think me gone; I'll come in mask.
Let me wait but one day, capricious love!

ROXANE.   But if 'tis known, your glory—

DE GUICHE.   Bah!

ROXANE.   The siege—

    Arras—

DE GUICHE.   So much the worse. Pray let me!

ROXANE.   No!

DE GUICHE.   Yes!

ROXANE *(tenderly).*   I should forbid you!

DE GUICHE.   Ah!

ROXANE.   Go!

(Aside.)   Christian stays.

                      (Aloud.)

I would have you a hero—Antony!

DE GUICHE.   Heavenly   word!   So you admire him?

ROXANE.   For him my heart has thrilled.

DE GUICHE.   Ah, well, I go!

(Kisses her hand.)   Are you content?

ROXANE.   Yes, my friend!

                  (He goes out.)

THE DUENNA *(making him a mock courtesy behind his
    back)*   Yes, my friend!

ROXANE *(to the Duenna).*

Let us be silent over what I've done.
Cyrano'ld take it ill to think I'd robbed him
Of going to the war.

(Calls towards the house.)   Cousin!

Scene III.

Roxane, the Duenna, Cyrano.

ROXANE.   We're going
   To Clomire's.
                    (*Points to the door opposite.*)
   There'll be speeches by Alcandre
   And Lysimon!
THE DUENNA (*putting her little finger in her ear*).   Yes!
      But my little finger
   Says we shall miss them!
CYRANO (*to Roxane*).   Do not miss these wonders!
         (*They arrive in front of Clomire's door.*)
THE DUENNA (*with rapture*).
   Oh, see! The knocker's wrapped with linen cloths.
                    (*To the knocker.*)
   So you are muffled, that your iron clang
   May not disturb their discourse—wicked child!
      (*Raises it with infinite care and raps softly.*)
ROXANE (*seeing the door open*).
   Let us go in!
(*From the threshold, to Cyrano.*) Let Christian wait for
      me,
   If he comes here, as I suppose he will.
CYRANO (*quickly, as she is about to disappear*).   Ah!
(*She turns back.*) On what do you intend to question
      him,
   To-day, after your habit?
ROXANE.   On—
CYRANO (*quickly*).   On what?
ROXANE.   But you'll be silent on it!
CYRANO.   Like a wall.

ROXANE. On nothing!—I shall tell him, "Loose the reins!
    Improvise; talk of love. Be glorious!"
CYRANO (*smiling*).   Good!
ROXANE.   Hush!
CYRANO.   Hush!
ROXANE.   Not a word!
            (*Goes in and shuts the door.*)
CYRANO (*bowing to her, after the door is shut*).   Accept
    my thanks!
(*The door opens again and Roxane puts out her head.*)
ROXANE.   He would prepare himself—
CYRANO.   Oh, no!
BOTH TOGETHER.   Hush!—
                (*The door closes.*)
CYRANO (*calling*).   Christian!

Scene IV.

Cryano, Christian.

CYRANO. I know just what is needed. Give good heed,
    This is your chance for glory. Lose no time,
    Make no objections. Quickly let us go
    To where you lodge. And I will teach you—
CHRISTIAN.   No!
CYRANO.   What?
CHRISTIAN.   No, I wait for Roxane here.
CYRANO.   What madness
    Has seized upon you? Come and quickly learn—
CHRISTIAN. I tell you no! I'm sick of borrowing
    Letters and speeches, playing this timid part.
    'Twas good at first! But now I feel she loves me!

Thanks, I am not afraid, I'll speak myself.

CYRANO.   Ah!

CHRISTIAN.   And who will say that I shall not know how?
  I'm not so stupid after all. You'll see!
  Besides, my friend, I've learned a deal from you.
  I can speak quite alone! And by the gods,
  One thing I can do, take her in my arms!—
  (*Seeing Roxane as she comes out of Clomire's house.*)
  'Tis she! No, do not leave me, Cyrano!

CYRANO (*bowing to him*). Speak quite alone, sir.
           (*Disappears behind the garden wall.*)

Scene V.

Christian, Roxane; the Duenna, for a moment.

ROXANE (*coming out of Clomire's house, with a number
       of people of whom she takes her leave, courtesies
       and bows*). Barthénoïde! Alcandre!

THE DUENNA (*in distress*). We missed the discourse on
       the Tender Passion!
              (*Returns to Roxane's house.*)

ROXANE (*still bowing*).
   Grémionë! Urimédonte! Adieu!
  (*All bow to Roxane, and to each other, separate, and
  depart by different streets. Roxane sees Christian.*)
   'Tis you!
              (*Goes to him.*)
   The evening falls. Wait. They are gone.
   The air is soft. No one is near. Sit down.
   Speak. I am listening.

CHRISTIAN (*sits by her on the bench. A pause*).   I love you.

ROXANE (*closing her eyes*).   Yes,
   Talk about love.
CHRISTIAN.   I love thee!
ROXANE.   'Tis the theme,
   Embroider it.
CHRISTIAN.   I love thee!
ROXANE.   Yes!
CHRISTIAN.   So much!
ROXANE.   Of course, and then—
CHRISTIAN.   And then—I'd be so glad
   If you loved me!— Tell me, Roxane, you do!
ROXANE (*with a little grimace*).
   You offer gruel when I hoped for sweets!
   Explain a little how you love!
CHRISTIAN.   But—much!
ROXANE.   Untwine your feelings from this single string!
CHRISTIAN.   Your neck!—I should so like to kiss it!
ROXANE.   Christian!
CHRISTIAN.   I love you.
ROXANE (*starting to get up*).   Once again!
CHRISTIAN (*quickly, holding her back*). I love you not!
ROXANE (*sitting down again*).
   'Tis fortunate!
CHRISTIAN.   I worship you!
ROXANE (*getting up and going away*).   Oh.
CHRISTIAN.   Yes!
   I grow a fool.
ROXANE (*drily*).   And that displeases me,
   Just as it would if you should ugly grow.
CHRISTIAN. But—
ROXANE.   Gather up your scattered eloquence.
CHRISTIAN.   I—
ROXANE.   I know; you love me. Good-bye.

CHRISTIAN.   Not at once!
  I'll tell you—
ROXANE (*opening the door to go in*).   That you worship
      me—I know.
  No! go away!
CHRISTIAN.   But I—
          (*She shuts the door in his face.*)
CYRANO (*who has come in unperceived a moment be-
      fore*).   'Tis a success!

Scene VI.

Christian, Cyrano; the Pages, for a moment.

CHRISTIAN.   Help!
CYRANO.   No, Sir!
CHRISTIAN.   I shall die unless at once
  I win her smiles again—
CYRANO.   And how the devil
  Can I teach you to do it on the spot?
CHRISTIAN (*seizing his arm*).
  Oh! come now, see!
      (*The window of the balcony is lighted up.*)
CYRANO (*with emotion*).   Her window!
CHRISTIAN.   I shall die!
CYRANO.   Lower your voice.
CHRISTIAN (*in very low voice*).   Shall die—
CYRANO.   The night is dark—
CHRISTIAN. Well?
CYRANO. It may be helped, though you do not deserve it.
  Take your position there, unhappy wight!
  Before the balcony ! I shall stand beneath

And prompt you with your words.

CHRISTIAN.   But—

CYRANO.   Hold your tongue.

THE PAGES *(reappearing in the background, to Cyrano).*
   Holloa!

CYRANO.   Hush!—
            (Signals to them to speak low).

FIRST PAGE *(in a low voice).*   We've just given Montfleury.

   His serenade—

CYRANO *(aside, quickly).*   Go, put yourselves in ambush.
   One at this end the street, the other there,
   And if some inconvenient passer comes
   Then play a tune.

SECOND PAGE.   What tune, Gassendi's pupil?

CYRANO.   Gay for a woman, mournful for a man.

*(The pages disappear, one at each end of the street. To
   Christian.)* Call her!

CHRISTIAN.   Roxane!

CYRANO *(picking up some pebbles and throwing them at
   the panes).*

   Wait till I throw a pebble.

ROXANE *(half opening the window).*

   Who calls me?

CHRISTIAN.   I.

ROXANE.   Who?

CHRISTIAN.   Christian.

ROXANE *(with disdain).*   Is it you?

CHRISTIAN.   I would speak with you.

CYRANO *(under the balcony).*   Good! Good! Almost
   whisper.

ROXANE.   Oh, no! You speak too ill. Begone!

CHRISTIAN.   I beg you!—

ROXANE.   No, you love me no longer.

CHRISTIAN (*Cyrano prompting him.*) What a charge!—
Ye gods!—to love no more—when—I love most!

ROXANE (*stopping, as she was about to close the window*).   That's better!

CHRISTIAN (*same action*). Love grows—cradled in my
soul—
My troubled soul—the which this cruel babe
Has taken for his cot.

ROXANE (*coming out on the balcony*). That's better now!
But since this love is cruel, you were foolish
That in his cot you did not smother him.

CHRISTIAN (*same action*).
That did I try—but the attempt was vain;
This new-born babe—is a little—Hercules.[3]

ROXANE.   That's better!

CHRISTIAN (*same action*).   So that in a trice—he stran-
gled
The serpents—Pride and—Doubt.

ROXANE (*leaning on the balcony rail*). That's very good.
But why with halting accents do you speak?
Your fancy's lame?

CYRANO (*pulling Christian under the balcony and glid-
ing into his place*).   Hush! This becomes too
hard.

ROXANE.   To-day your words are faltering. Why is this?

CYRANO (*talking in an undertone, like Christian*).
Because it now is night; and in the dark
They grope about, striving to find your ear.

ROXANE.   But mine encounter no such obstacles.

CYRANO.   They find their way at once? That is not
strange,
Because 'tis in my heart that I receive them—

My heart is large—your ear is wondrous small.
Besides, your words descend; their pace is swift,
While mine must climb, madame, a longer task.

ROXANE.   But they climb better in these last few moments.

CYRANO.   As they have practised, they have learned the
   way.

ROXANE.   Truly, 'tis from a height I speak to you.

CYRANO.   And you would kill me, if you should let fall
   From such a height, a hard word on my heart.

ROXANE (*with a motion*).   I'm coming down.

CYRANO (*quickly*).   No!

ROXANE (*showing him the bench which is under the balcony*).

   Climb upon the bench.
   Quickly!

CYRANO (*drawing back with alarm into the darkness*).
   No!

ROXANE.   What?—No?

CYRANO (*his feelings gaining on him more and more*).
   For a moment let me
   Improve this chance which offers—to be able
   To talk in accents soft, but not to see.

ROXANE.   But not to see?

CYRANO.   Yes, 'tis a sheer delight;
   We guess at one another in the dark,
   You see the blackness of a trailing cloak,
   I see the whiteness of a summer robe,
   And I am but a shadow, you a radiance.
   You know not what these moments mean for me!
   If ever I was eloquent—

ROXANE.   You were!

CYRANO.   Until this hour my words have never come
   From my own heart—

ROXANE. Why?

CYRANO. Because, until now
  I spoke through—

ROXANE. What?

CYRANO. —the dizziness where swims
  Whome'er you look on— But to-night it seems
  That for the first time I shall speak to you.

ROXANE. 'T is true that you have quite another voice.

CYRANO (*drawing near, feverishly*).
  Yes, quite another, for in the sheltering night
  I dare at last to be myself—I dare—
        (*Stops, and in bewilderment.*)
  What was I saying—I know not—All of this—
  Forgive my mounting passion—is so sweet—
  And is so new for me.

ROXANE. So new?

CYRANO (*distracted and still trying to take back his
    words*).
  So new—
  —Why, yes!—to be sincere—without constraint,
  The fear of being mocked has wrung my heart.

ROXANE. Mocked about what?

CYRANO. Oh—but—about my ardor—
  My heart for shame has ever clothed itself
  With wit as with a garment. I start forth
  To snatch a star from out the sky,—I stop
  In fear of ridicule,—and pluck a flower.

ROXANE. The flower has charms.

CYRANO. This evening let us scorn it.

ROXANE. You never yet have talked to me like this!

CYRANO. Oh! far removed from Cupid's enginery
  'T is pleasant to escape to greener things.
  Instead of drinking from a golden thimble

Insipid syrups, slowly, drop by drop,
Shall we not let the soul allay its thirst
By drinking freely from the river's flood?

ROXANE. But your wit?

CYRANO. I used to make you stay.
But now to speak with a court poet's phrases
Would be to affront this night, these odors sweet,
This magic hour, and even Nature's self.
Let Heaven, with one glance of her gleaming stars,
Take away all our wonted artifice;
I fear, lest in our subtle alchemy
The heart's true feeling may go up in smoke,
The soul may spend itself in empty play,
And e'en refinement be refined to naught.

ROXANE. But your wit?

CYRANO. I hate, when it plays with love.
For when one truly loves, it is a crime
Too long to thrust and parry. The moment comes—
And those to whom it never comes I pity—
When in our hearts we feel a noble passion
Saddened by every clever phrase we turn.

ROXANE. If to us two this moment now has come,
What words will you speak to me?

CYRANO. Every word
That rises to my lips. I'll cast them all
Before you in a heap, with no arrangement—
I love you—I am smothered—I am mad
I love you—I am faint—it is too much;
Your name hangs in my heart like a bell's tongue,
And evermore, Roxane, with love I tremble,
And the bell swings, and then your name rings out.
And everything you do lives in my heart;
Last year there was one day I well remember,

The tenth of May, one morn you dressed your hair
So that its radiance burnt into my soul;
And just as he, who at the sun too long
Has gazed, sees circles red where'er he looks;
So when I left the flames in which I swam
My eyes saw blots of gold on everything.

ROXANE.   Yes, this indeed is love—

CYRANO.   Truly, this passion
Jealous and terrible, which sweeps me on,
Is love indeed, with all its mournful madness!
Is love indeed, and yet it is not selfish!
Ah, for your joy I'd gladly give my own,
Even if you should never know; if I
Might sometimes from afar hear the soft laugh
Of happiness born from my sacrifice,—
Your very look rouses new worth in me,
Do you begin to understand it now?
And feel my soul climb slowly through the dark?
Ah! but this night is all too fair, too sweet!
I say all this to you; and you, you listen;
It is too much. E'en in my maddest hopes
I never hoped so much. There's nothing left,
Except for me to die at once. She trembles,
There through the branches dark, and for my words,
For you are trembling, a leaf among the leaves,
For thou art trembling, and I plainly felt
Whether thou wouldst or no, the trembling dear
Of thy sweet hand descend the jasmine branch.
(Madly kisses the end of a hanging branch.)

ROXANE.   I tremble, I weep, I love thee, I am thine—
Aye, drunk with love!

CYRANO.   Then let death come at once.
Since it is I who mixed the cup for thee!

I ask but one thing more—

CHRISTIAN *(under the balcony).* A kiss!

ROXANE *(drawing back).* What?

CYRANO. Oh!

ROXANE. You're asking?

CYRANO. Yes—I—

(To Christian, aside.) You go far too fast!

CHRISTIAN. Since she is moved, I must improve my
    chance!

CYRANO *(to Roxane).*

  Yes, I—I asked, 'tis true, but, gracious heavens!

  I understand, I was too bold by far.

ROXANE *(somewhat disappointed).*

  You insist no more than that?

CYRANO. Yes, I insist—

  Without insisting. Yes! Your modesty

  Is saddened—Well, this kiss—grant me it not.

CHRISTIAN *(to Cyrano, pulling his cloak).*

  Why?

CYRANO. Hush, Christian.

ROXANE *(leaning over).* What do you say so low?

CYRANO. I scold myself for having gone too far,

  And to myself I said, "Hush, Christian."

(The lutes begin to play.) Wait!

  Some one is coming.

*(Roxane closes the window. Cyrano listens to the lutes,
  one of which plays a lively air, the other a mournful
                    one.)*

  Sad? Gay? What's their plan?

  Is it a man, or woman?—'tis a monk!

  *(A Capuchin enters, going from house to house,
    lantern in hand, looking at the doors.)*

Scene VII.

Cyrano, Christian, a Capuchin. —the monk

CYRANO (*to the Capuchin*).
    Who's this new follower of Diogenes?[24]
THE CAPUCHIN.   I'm looking for the house—
CHRISTIAN.   He's in our way!
THE CAPUCHIN.   Of Madame Madeleine Robin.
CHRISTIAN.   What's he after?
CYRANO (*showing him a street leading away*).
    This way, keep to the right,—still to the right.
THE CAPUCHIN.   Thank you! I'll say for you a *pater noster.*[5]
                        (*Goes out.*)
CYRANO.   Good luck. My prayers accompany your cowl![6]
                        (*Comes back to Christian.*)

Scene VIII.

Cyrano, Christian.

CHRISTIAN.   Get me this kiss!—
CYRANO.   No!
CHRISTIAN.   Soon or late—
CYRANO.   'Tis true!
    'T will come; this moment of supreme delight
    When your two mouths together shall be drawn
    Because of her red lips, and your moustache.
                        (*To himself.*)
    I'd rather that it were because—
(*Noise of shutters reopening. Christian hides under the
                        balcony.*)

Scene IX.

Cyrano, Christian, Roxane.

ROXANE (*coming forward on the balcony*).
　　'T is you?
　　We were speaking of—of—of a—
CYRANO.　　Of a kiss.
　　The word is sweet, I see not why your lips
　　So fear to speak it; if it burns them now
　　What will it be itself? Be not afraid.
　　Make not a terror of it. Did you not,
　　Just now, unknowingly, without alarm,
　　Leave off your mockery, and softly pass
　　From sigh to sigh, and from a sigh to tears?
　　Pass on yet further by the easy path—
　　'Twixt tears and kiss there's but a moment's tremble.
ROXANE.　　Be still!
CYRANO.　　A kiss, when all is said, what is it?
　　An oath sworn nearer by; a promise made
　　With greater certainty; a vow which seeks
　　To make itself more binding; a rosy dot
　　Placed on the "i" in loving; 'tis a secret
　　Told to the mouth instead of to the ear;
　　A moment of the infinite, which makes
　　A sound like to the humming of bees' wings;
　　A greeting like the sweet breath of a flower;
　　A way to feel the heart beat for a space,
　　And taste the soul a moment on the lips.
ROXANE.　　Be still!
CYRANO.　　A kiss, madame, it is so noble
　　That e'en the Queen of France, the Queen herself,
　　Let her most happy courtier take one!

ROXANE.   Well!

CYRANO *(growing more impassioned).*
  Like Buckingham, I've suffered silent pangs;
  Like him, a Queen I worship—you, my Queen.
  Like him, I'm sad and faithful.

ROXANE.   And like him
  You're fair.

CYRANO *(aside, sobered).*   True, I am fair, I quite for-
    got.

ROXANE. Well, climb and pluck this flower without a
    peer!

CYRANO *(pushing Christian towards the balcony).*
  Climb!

ROXANE.   This heart beat.

CYRANO.   Climb!

ROXANE.   This humming of bees' wings.

CYRANO.   Climb!

CHRISTIAN *(hesitating).*   But now it seems perhaps I'd
    better not!

ROXANE.   This moment of the infinite.

CYRANO *(pushing him).*   Climb, fool!
    *(Christian plunges forward, and by means of the
    bench, the branches, and the pillars reaches the
        balustrade,[8] which he vaults.)*

CHRISTIAN.   Ah! Roxane!
        (Embraces her and bends over her lips.)

CYRANO.   Ah! My heart, what torture strange!
  Kiss, feast of love where I am Lazarus,[7]
  There reach me in the dark some crumbs from thee;
  But still I feel my heart has something gained
  Since on these lips where Roxane now is caught
  It is the words I spoke just now she kisses.
        (The lutes are heard.)

Now sad, now gay, the Capuchin!
*(Pretends to run as if he were arriving from a distance
and calls in a loud voice.)*

Holloa!

ROXANE. What is it?

CYRANO. It is I, I was just passing—
Christian's still there?

CHRISTIAN *(greatly astonished).* What, Cyrano?

ROXANE. Good evening,
Cousin!

CYRANO. Good evening, cousin!

ROXANE. I'm coming down.
*(Disappears in the house. The Capuchin re-enters in
the background.)*

CHRISTIAN *(seeing him).* Again!

Scene X.

Cyrano, Christian, Roxane, the Capuchin, Ragueneau.

THE CAPUCHIN. 'T is here—I'm sure—Madeleine Robin!

CYRANO. You said Ro-*lin.*

THE CAPUCHIN. No, *Bin:* B, i, n, *bin!*

ROXANE *(appearing on the threshold of the house, followed by Ragueneau carrying a lantern, and by
Christian).* What is it?

THE CAPUCHIN. A letter.

CHRISTIAN. What?

THE CAPUCHIN *(to Roxane).* Oh! It must be
About some holy matter. It was a lord,
A worthy lord who—

ROXANE. 'T is De Guiche!

CHRISTIAN.   He dares?—

ROXANE.   Oh, but he will not trouble me forever.
                    (Unsealing the letter.)
    I love you, and if—
*(She reads by the light of Ragueneau's lantern, aside in
        a low voice.)* "Mademoiselle—
    The drums
    Beat loud, my soldiers buckle on their tunics;
    They go, 'tis thought that I am gone; I stay,
    I disobey you. I am in this convent.
    I am coming and I warn you of it first,
    By a monk who is as simple as a lamb,
    And who knows naught of this. Your lips have smiled
    Just now too kindly on me; I have wished
    To see them once again. Bid all begone,
    And graciously receive a man too bold,
    And yet already pardoned, may I hope?
    Who signs himself your very humble—"
(To the Capuchin.)   Father,
    Here's what this letter tells me, listen to it:
                (All draw near, she reads aloud.)
    "Mademoiselle,
    We must submit ourselves
    To the Cardinal's will, hard though it be for you;
    And that is why I've chosen a Capuchin,
    Very discreet, intelligent, and holy,
    To send this letter unto your fair hands.
    We wish that he should give you, at your dwelling,
    At once, the Church's blessing—
(turns the page)   —on your marriage.
    Christian must secretly become your husband.
    I send him. You dislike him. Be resigned.
    Bethink yourself that heaven will bless your zeal,

And be assured again, Mademoiselle,
Of his respect who is, and ever will be,
Your very humble, very—*et cœtera*."

THE CAPUCHIN. The worthy lord! I had no fear; I said so.
It could be only on some holy errand.

ROXANE (*aside to Christian*). Do I read letters well?

CHRISTIAN. Hum!

ROXANE (*aloud, in despair*). Ah! 'T is frightful.

THE CAPUCHIN (*turning the light of his lantern on Cyrano*).
Is it you?

CHRISTIAN. It is I!

THE CAPUCHIN (*turning the light towards him and apparently seized with doubts, when he sees his good looks*).
But why—

ROXANE (*quickly*). Post scriptum.
"Give for the convent six score gold pistoles."

THE CAPUCHIN. A worthy, worthy lord!
(*To Roxane.*) Resign yourself.

ROXANE (*like a martyr*).
I am resigned.
(*While Ragueneau opens the doors to the Capuchin, whom Christian invites to enter, she says aside to Cyrano.*)
You make De Guiche wait here.
He's coming—let him not come in before—

CYRANO. I understand.
(*To the Capuchin.*) To bless them takes how long?

THE CAPUCHIN. A quarter of an hour.

CYRANO (*pushing them all towards the house*).
Go, I stay.

ROXANE (*to Christian*).
Come.

                    (*They go in.*)

CYRANO.   How to make De Guiche lose fifteen minutes?
  (*Rushes to the bench and climbs up the wall towards
                    the balcony.*)
    There! Let us climb—my plan is made—
(*The lutes begin to play a doleful bar.*) Holloa!

— Hello

    It is a man!
                    (*The tremolo becomes mournful.*)
    Ho! ho. This time it is one!
(*He is on the balcony, pulls his hat over his eyes, takes
    off his sword, then leans forward and looks out.*)
    No, it is not too high.
(*He vaults the balustrade, and drawing towards him
  the long branch of one of the trees which border the
wall of the garden, he grasps it with both hands, ready
                    to let himself fall.*)
    This atmosphere
    I am about to trouble.

                    Scene XI.

Cyrano, De Guiche.

DE GUICHE   (*entering, masked, feeling his way in the
        night*).
    What is this cursèd Capuchin about?
CYRANO.   The deuce, my voice?—If he should recog-
        nize it?
    (*Letting go with one hand, he pretends to turn an
                    invisible key.*)
    Cric, crac!
(*Solemnly.*) Speak like a Gascon, Cyrano.

DE GUICHE (*looking at the house*).

'Tis there! I cannot see. This mask annoys me.

(*Starts to go in. Cyrano leaps from the balcony, holding on to the branch, which bends, and lands him between De Guiche and the door; he pretends to fall heavily, as if from a great distance, and flattens out on the ground, where he remains motionless, as if stunned. De Guiche jumps backward.*)

Hah! What!

(*When he lifts his eyes, the branch has swung back; he sees only the sky; he does not understand.*)

Whence falls this man here?

CYRANO (*sitting up, and speaking with a Gascon accent*).

From the moon.

DE GUICHE. From the——?

CYRANO (*in a dreamy voice*). What time is it?

DE GUICHE. He's lost his mind.

CYRANO. What country? What o'clock? What day? What season?

DE GUICHE. But——

CYRANO. I am dazed.

DE GUICHE, Monsieur——

CYRANO. For like a bomb

I've fallen from the moon!

DE GUICHE (*impatient*). Yes, but Monsieur!——

CYRANO (*getting up, with a terrible voice*).

Thence have I fallen!

DE GUICHE (*drawing back*). Yes, yes, thence you fell!
    ——Perhaps he is a madman.

CYRANO (*advancing towards him*). And my fall,——

It is no metaphor!

DE GUICHE. But——

CYRANO.   A century since.
Or else a moment—in my fall I lost
All track of time,—I was in that yellow ball!

DE GUICHE (*shrugging his shoulders*).
Yes, let me pass.

CYRANO (*standing in his way*).
Where am I? Tell me frankly
Keep nothing hid! In what place, in what spot,
Monsieur, have I just fallen like a meteor?

DE GUICHE.   The Devil!

CYRANO.   As I fell I could not choose
My landing-place—I know not where I fell!—
And is it to a moon or to a world,
Whither my weight has just now drawn me down?

DE GUICHE.   But, sir, I tell you—

CYRANO (*with a cry of terror which makes De Guiche draw back*).
Ha! Ye gods! Meseems
That in this country folk have faces black!

DE GUICHE (*raising his hand to his face*).
What?

CYRANO (*with a distinct show of fear*).
Am I in Algiers?[9] Are you a native?

DE GUICHE (*who has felt his mask*).
This mask—

CYRANO (*pretending to be somewhat reassured*).
I'm then in Genoa or Venice?

DE GUICHE (*trying to pass*).
A lady waits me—

CYRANO (*wholly reassured*).   Then I am in Paris!

DE GUICHE (*smiling in spite of himself*).
He's an amusing fellow.

CYRANO.   Ah! You laugh?

DE GUICHE.   I laugh, but wish to pass.

CYRANO (*beaming*).   Indeed, 'tis Paris!

(*Entirely at his ease, smiling, brushing himself, and
bowing.*)

I came—excuse me—by the latest whirlwind.
The ether clings to me. I've travelled far!
My eyes are filled with star-dust. On my spurs
I still have shreds torn from a planet's hide!

(*Picking something from his sleeve.*)

See, on my doublet, there's a comet's hair!

(*Puffs as if to blow it away.*)

DE GUICHE (*beside himself*).

Monsieur!—

CYRANO (*just as he starts to pass, holds out his leg as if to
show him something, and stops him*).

And in my leg I bring a tooth
From the Great Bear,[10]—and as I passed the Trident.[11]
Trying to dodge one of its three sharp prongs,
I fell, and landed seated on the Scales,
Whose needle at this moment marks my weight.

(*Quickly preventing De Guiche from passing, and
taking him by the button of his doublet.*)

If you should press my nose between your fingers,
It would spurt milk!—

DE GUICHE.   What? Milk?

CYRANO.   From the Milky Way!

DE GUICHE.   Oh, by the lords of Hell!—

CYRANO.   'T is Heaven that sends me!

(*Folding his arms.*) Now, would you think, I saw it as I
fell,—

That Sirius,[12] at night, puts on a cap?

(*Confidentially.*) The other Bear is still too small to bite.

(*Smiling.*) And as I crossed the Lyre, I broke a string.

(Proudly.) But I shall write a book about it all,
      And the golden stars, that in my scorchèd cloak
      I brought away at my own risk and peril,
      Will serve as asterisks when it is printed.

DE GUICHE.   Finally, I insist—

CYRANO.   I catch your meaning!

DE GUICHE.   Monsieur!

CYRANO.   You wish to hear from my own mouth
      Of what the moon is made, and if folk dwell
      Within the roundness of this strange alembic?

DE GUICHE.   No! No! I wish—

CYRANO.   To know how I ascended?
      'Twas by a means that I devised myself.

DE GUICHE *(discouraged)*.   He's mad!

CYRANO *(scornfully)*.   I did not use the stupid eagle.
      Of Regiomontanus,[13] nor the pigeon Archytas[14] used—

DE GUICHE. Mad!—but a learnèd madman!

CYRANO.   I followed naught that had been done be-
      fore.

*(De Guiche has succeeded in passing, and is striding
towards Roxane's door. Cyrano follows him, ready to
                  lay hold of him.)*

      Six ways did I devise to violate
      The virgin Azure!

DE GUICHE *(turning)*.   Six?

CYRANO *(volubly)*.   I deck my body,
      Naked as on the day that I was born,
      With crystal phials filled up to the brim,
      With tears dropped from the morning sky, and then
      Expose me to the full blaze of the sun,
      Which draws me up the while it drinks the dew.

DE GUICHE *(surprised and taking a step towards Cyrano)*.
      Yes, that makes one.

CYRANO (*drawing back to get him on the other side*).
 And this too I could do:
 Produce a whirlwind, and so take my flight,—
 By rarefying air in a cedar chest
 With burning mirrors in an icosahedron.[15]
DE GUICHE (*taking another step*). Two!
CYRANO (*still drawing back*).
 Or, having skill of hand as well as brain,
 On a grasshopper made with springs of steel,
 Dart, with successive blasts of powder fired,
 Through the blue pastures where the stars are grazing.
DE GUICHE (*following him without suspecting it, and
  counting on his fingers*).
 Three!
CYRANO. And since all smoke must surely rise aloft,
 Blow in a globe enough to bear me up.
DE GUICHE (*same action, more and more amazed*).
 Four!
CYRANO. Since Diana,[16] when her bow is smallest,
 Loves, oh, ye oxen, to suck out your marrow!—
 To anoint myself withal!
DE GUICHE (*in stupefaction*). Five!
CYRANO (*who, while talking to him has led him to the
  other side of the street, near a bench*).
 Finally,
 Placing myself upon a plate of iron,
 I take a magnet, and throw it in the air!
 'Tis a good way—the iron rushes on
 Fast as the magnet flies, and follows after.
 Again I throw the magnet—there you are!
 In this way I ascend without a limit.
DE GUICHE. Six! These be six good ways. What system,
  sir,

Of the six did you choose?

CYRANO.   I chose a seventh.

DE GUICHE.   Really, what is it?

CYRANO.   You could never guess!

DE GUICHE.   This rascal's growing interesting now.

CYRANO (*making the noise of the waves, with great, mys-
          terious gestures*).

Hooüh! Hooüh!

DE GUICHE.   Well?

CYRANO.   You guess?

DE GUICHE.   No.

CYRANO.   The tide!

At the hour when the moon doth draw the wave
I lay upon the sand,—after a bath,—
And the head led the way, my friend, because
The hair keeps so much water in its locks.
I rose in air, up, straight up, like an angel,
I ascended gently, softly, with no effort,
When suddenly I felt a shock,—then—

DE GUICHE (*carried away by curiosity, sitting down on
          the bench*).   Then?

CYRANO.   Then (*resuming his natural voice*),
The quarter hour has passed. I let you go.
The marriage is made.

DE GUICHE (*getting up with a bound*). What! Come! Am
          I then drunk?
This voice?
(*The door of the house opens, and lackeys appear,
carrying lighted candelabra. Light. Cyrano takes off
          his hat with its lowered brim.*)
This nose! Cyrano?

CYRANO (*bowing*).   Cyrano.
This very moment they've exchanged the rings.

DE GUICHE. Who are they?

(He turns—Tableau. Behind the lackeys, Roxane and Christian hold hands. The Capuchin follows them, smiling. Ragueneau also holds a torch. The duenna closes the line, in great confusion, dressed in a wrapper). Heavens!

Scene XII.

The same, Roxane, Christian, the Capuchin, Ragueneau, Lackeys, the Duenna.

DE GUICHE *(to Roxane).* You!
        (Recognizing Christian with stupefaction).
    He?
(Bowing to Roxane with admiration.) A clever stroke!
(To Cyrano.) My compliments, inventor of machines!
    Your story would have made a saint stop short
    At heaven's gate. Remember the details,
    For it might well be turned into a book.
CYRANO *(bowing).*
    Sir, that's advice that I engage to follow.
THE CAPUCHIN *(showing the lovers to De Guiche, and wagging his great white beard with satisfaction).*
    A handsome pair, my son, joined there by you!
DE GUICHE *(giving him a frigid glance).* Yes.
(To Roxane). Be kind enough, Madame, to bid your husband
    Farewell.
ROXANE. Why so?
DE GUICHE *(to Christian).* The troops are on the march.
    Go join your regiment!

ROXANE.   To go to war?

DE GUICHE.   Of course.

ROXANE.   But the Cadets, sir, do not go.

DE GUICHE.   They'll go.
    (*Drawing out the paper he had in his pocket.*)
    Here is the order.
(*To Christian*).   Take it, Baron!

ROXANE (*throwing herself into Christian's arms*).
    Christian!

DE GUICHE (*sneeringly, to Cyrano*).
    The wedding night is still far off!

CYRANO (*aside*).   To think that he believes that greatly
    pains me!

CHRISTIAN (*to Roxane*).   Your lips again!

CYRANO.   Come, come, that is enough!

CHRISTIAN (*continuing to embrace Roxane*).
    'Tis hard to leave her. You know not—

CYRANO (*trying to draw him away*).   Yes, I know.
    (*Drums beating a march are heard in the distance.*)

DE GUICHE (*who has retired to the background*).
    The regiment is off!

ROXANE (*to Cyrano, holding back Christian whom
    Cyrano still tries to draw away*).
    I trust him to you!
    O promise me that naught shall put his life
    In danger.

CYRANO.   I shall try—but cannot promise.

ROXANE (*same action*).
    And promise that he shall be very careful!

CYRANO.   Yes, I shall try, but—

ROXANE.   In this fearful siege,
    That he shall ne'er be cold.

CYRANO.   I'll do my best

But—
ROXANE (*same action*).   That he shall be faithful—
CYRANO.   Yes, of course,
    But—
ROXANE (*same action*).   That he shall write often!
CYRANO (*stopping himself*).   Ah! I promise!

CURTAIN.

Fourth Act

The Gascon Cadets.

*The station occupied by Carbon de Castel-Jaloux's com-
pany at the siege of Arras.¹ In the background, a rampart crossing the entire stage. Beyond is seen a plain
stretching away to the horizon; the country is covered
with earthworks. The walls of Arras, and its roofs, sil-
houetted against the sky, in the far distance. Tents; arms
scattered about, drums, etc. Day is about to dawn. The
east is yellow. Sentinels stationed at intervals. Camp-
fires. The Gascon Cadets are asleep, wrapped in their
cloaks. Carbon de Castel-Jaloux and Le Bret are on
watch. They are pale and very thin. Christian is asleep
among the rest, wrapped in his cape, in the foreground,
his face lit by the firelight. Silence.*

Scene I.

Christian, Carbon de Castel-Jaloux, Le Bret, the
    Cadets; afterwards Cyrano.

LE BRET.   'T is frightful!

CARBON.   Frightful!

LE BRET.   Lord!

CARBON (*making a sign to him to speak lower*).
   Swear in a whisper.
   You'll waken them. (*To the Cadets.*) Hush! Sleep. (*To
      Le Bret.*) He who sleeps, dines!

LE BRET.   When one is sleepless, 't is lean fare enough.
   What famine!
      (*Scattering shots heard in the distance.*)

CARBON.   Curses on these wretched shots!
   They will awake my lads. (*To the Cadets, who raise
      their heads.*) Sleep on!
   (*They settle down again. More shots, nearer.*)

A CADET (*moving*).   The deuce!
   Again?

CARBON   'T is nothing. Cyrano returns.
      (*The heads which had been lifted fall again.*)

A SENTINEL (*without*).
   Halt! Who goes there?

CYRANO'S VOICE.   I! Bergerac!

THE SENTINEL ON THE RAMPART.   The devil!
   Who's there?

CYRANO (*appearing on top of the rampart*).
   Bergerac, fool!

LE BRET.   Ah, thank the Lord!

CYRANO (*making a sign to him to awake no one*).
   Hush!

LE BRET.   Wounded?

CYRANO   You know well they have a habit
   Of missing me each morning.

LE BRET.   'T is too much
   To risk your life to carry every day

A letter—

CYRANO *(stopping before Christian).*   But I gave my
    word he'd write.

(Looks at him.)   He sleeps. He has grown pale. If the
    poor child

    Knew how he dies of hunger—but always fair!

LE BRET.   Go straight to sleep.

CYRANO.   Now do not scold, Le Bret—

    Know this: that where I pass the Spanish lines

    I've chosen a spot where they are always drunk.

LE BRET.   Some day you should bring back some food
    for us.

CYRANO. I must go light to pass; and yet I know

    There'll be some news to-night. If I mistake not,

    The French will either eat or die.

LE BRET.   Tell on!

CYRANO.   No. I am not quite certain—you will see—

CARBON.   To die of hunger while one lays a siege

    Is sorry warfare.

LE BRET.   Ah! this siege of Arras

    Is a strange tangle, full of many knots:

    We besiege Arras;—caught in our own trap,

    The Cardinal-Prince of Spain besieges us.

CYRANO.   Some one should come to besiege him in
    turn.

LE BRET.   It is no laughing matter.

CYRANO.   Oh!

LE BRET.   To think

    That every day you risk a life like yours

    To carry—*(Seeing him turn towards a tent.)*

    Whither now?

CYRANO.   To write another!

        (Lifts the tent-flap and disappears.)

Scene II.

The Same; without Cyrano.

*(Day has just dawned. Rosy light. The town of Arras lies
    golden on the horizon. A cannon-shot is heard, fol-
    lowed immediately by a ruffle of drums, very distant,
    to the left. Other drums are heard near by. The
    drumbeats answer each other, and coming together
    almost burst upon the scene; then withdraw towards
    the right, going through the camp. Noises of awaken-
    ing. Distant voices of officers.)*

CARBON *(with a sigh)*.   The reveille—alas!

*(The Cadets move in their cloaks and stretch them-
    selves.)*   Nourishing sleep!

You cease; and what will be their cry I know

Only too well!

A CADET *(sitting up)*.   I'm hungry!

ANOTHER.   I am dying!

ALL.   Oh!

CARBON.   Get up!

THIRD CADET.   Not a movement!

FOURTH CADET.   Not a step!

THE FIRST *(looking at himself in a piece of his cuirass)*.

My tongue is yellow; this weather is unwholesome!

ANOTHER.   My badge of barony for a bit of cheese!

ANOTHER.   If no one will provide for my poor stomach

Something on which the chyle² may do its work,

Achilles-like, I'll sulk within my tent.

ANOTHER.   Bread!

CARBON *(going into the tent into which Cyrano had en-
    tered: in a low voice)*.

Cyrano!

OTHERS. We're dying!

CARBON *(still in a low voice, at the door of the tent).*
  To our aid!
  You who can always answer them so gaily,
  Come, cheer them up!

SECOND CADET *(rushing at the first, who is chewing
    something).* What are you nibbling on?

THE FIRST. On cannon-wadding, fried with axle-grease,
  Cooked in a helmet. There is not much game
  Here around Arras.

ANOTHER *(entering).* I'm just from the hunt.

ANOTHER *(same action).*
  And in the river Scarpe I have been fishing.

ALL *(standing and rushing upon the last comers).*
  What have you got—a pheasant, or a carp?
  Come, show them quickly!

THE FISHERMAN. A gudgeon.

THE HUNTER. And a sparrow.

ALL *(exasperated).*
  Enough! Let's mutiny.

CARBON. Help, Cyrano!
            (It is now broad day.)

Scene III.

The Same; Cyrano.

CYRANO *(coming out of his tent, placid, a pen over his
    ear, a book in his hand).* Well?
(Silence. To the first Cadet.)
  Why are you walking with this lagging step?

THE CADET. I've something in my heels which troubles
    me.

CYRANO.   And what is that?

THE CADET.   My stomach.

CYRANO.   So have I.

THE CADET.   Does it not trouble you?

CYRANO.   It makes me tall.

SECOND CADET. I have long teeth.

CYRANO.   You'll get the bigger bite.

A THIRD.   My stomach's hollow.

CYRANO.   We'll use it for a drum.

ANOTHER.   And as for me, I've buzzings in my ears.

CYRANO.   No, no! A famished stomach, not your ears!

ANOTHER.   Oh, to eat something—dressed with oil!

CYRANO (*taking off the Cadet's helmet and putting it in his hand*).   Your *sallet!*[3]

ANOTHER.   Is there naught to devour?

CYRANO (*tossing him the book he holds in his hand*).
     Try my Homer![4]

ANOTHER.   The Minister at home has four good meals.

CYRANO.   Should he send you a partridge?

THE SAME.   Well, why not?
     And wine.

CYRANO.   Some Burgundy, Richelieu, if you please!

THE SAME.   By some good Capuchin.

CYRANO.   His highness grey?

ANOTHER.   I'm hungry as a bear.

CYRANO.   Eat your own fat then!

FIRST CADET (*shrugging his shoulders*).
     That is your way—to jest, to score your point.

CYRANO.   Ah, yes, the jest, the point!—and well I hope
     That I may die some night, 'neath rosy skies,
     For a good cause, and making a good jest.
     Oh, to fall by the only noble weapon,
     Struck by a foeman worthy of one's self,—

Fall on the field of glory, not the sick-bed,
With point in heart, as well as on one's lips!
CRY OF ALL.   I'm hungry!
CYRANO (*crossing his arms*).
   Shame! you think of naught but food.
   Come, Bertrandou, the fifer, once a shepherd,
   Take from its leathern case one of your fifes.
   Blow! and play for this pack of lazy gluttons
   The old airs of our home, that hold us fast,—
   In which each note is like a little sister;
   In which are caught the tones of voices dear—
   Airs sweet and slow, like to the curling smoke
   That rises from the village of our birth,—
   These melodies which speak our native tongue.
   (*The old man sits down and prepares his fife.*)
   And let the warlike fife, that grieves to-day,
   Bethink itself a moment—while your fingers
   Dance up and down its length like darting birds—
   That ere 'twas wrought of ebony, 'twas a reed;
   And let it marvel at its song, and find
   Sweet memories of its peaceful, rustic youth.
(*The old man begins to play airs of the South of France.*)
   List, Gascons,—'neath his fingers 'tis no longer
   The camp's shrill fife, it is the forest's flute;
   And from his lips no battle-blast is blown,
   'T is the slow whistle of our humble goatherds.
   List, Gascons,—'tis the vale, the plain, the forest;
   The sunbrowned herdsman with his bonnet red;
   The Dordogne,[5] with its evenings green and sweet.
   List, Gascons,—'tis the whole of Gascony!
   (*All heads are bowed; all eyes are dreamy. Tears are
   furtively wiped away on the backs of sleeves and
   corners of cloaks.*)

CARBON (*to Cyrano, aside*).   But you have made them
    weep.
CYRANO.   Only homesickness.
    A nobler ill than hunger: mind, not body.
    'T is well their pains should strike another organ,
    And that it is their hearts which now are wrung.
CARBON.   But when you touch their hearts you weaken
    them.
CYRANO (*signalling to the drummer to approach*).
    Withhold your blame. The courage in their blood
    Awakens quickly. 'T is enough—
    (*Makes a gesture. The drum is sounded.*)
ALL (*rising and rushing to arms*).   What! What!
CYRANO (*smiling*).
    One ruffle of the drum's enough, you see.
    Farewell regrets, dreams, love,—and province old!
    The drum soon drives away what the fife brought!
A CADET (*looking into the distance*).
    Ah! There's Monsieur De Guiche.
ALL THE CADETS (*murmuring*).   Hoo!
CYRANO (*smiling*).   Flattering sound!
A CADET.   He wearies us!
ANOTHER.   With his great ruff of lace
    Over his armor—he comes to show it off.
ANOTHER.   It is like wearing cambric over steel.
THE FIRST.   It's good—if you have boils upon your neck.
THE SECOND.   A courtier still.
ANOTHER.   The nephew of his uncle.
CARBON.   Yet he's a Gascon.
THE FIRST.   Trust him not. He's false.
    Because the Gascons—really—should be mad.
    A Gascon with his wits is dangerous.
LE BRET.   He's pale.

ANOTHER.   He's hungry, like the rest of us.
   But since his armor's gay with silver-gilt
   His belly-pangs but sparkle in the sun.
CYRANO (*quickly*).
   Let us no longer seem to be in pain.
   Your cards, your pipes, your dice!—
   (*All quickly begin their games,—on the drums, on the
benches, and on their cloaks spread on the ground; and
          they light long pipes of tobacco.*)
   I read Descartes.[6]
(*Walks up and down, and reads a little book which he
   has taken out of his pocket. Tableau—De Guiche
enters; everyone seems absorbed and contented. He is
      very pale. He goes toward Carbon.*)

Scene IV.

The Same; De Guiche.

DE GUICHE (*to Carbon*).   Good day! (*They both look at
      each other.*) (*Aside, with satisfaction.*) He's turn-
      ing green.
CARBON (*same tone*).   He's naught but eyes.
DE GUICHE (*looking at the Cadets*).
   Are these the malcontents?—Yes, gentlemen,
   I hear I am lampooned on every side:
   And that, among your aristocracy
   Bred on a mountain-side, in Périgord
   Or Béarn, you cannot find hard words enough.
   For your commander,—calling me a trickster,
   A shallow courtier; that it troubles you
   To see a point-lace collar on my cuirass;
   And that you never cease to take it ill

That every Gascon need not be a beggar.
      (Silence. They play; they smoke.)
Shall I then have you punished by your Captain?
No!

CARBON.   I am free and give no punishments.

DE GUICHE.   Ah!

CARBON.   I've paid my company. It is my own:
And as a soldier only I obey.

DE GUICHE.   Indeed! That is enough.
(Addressing the Cadets.) I can despise
    Your mockery. You know how I stand fire.
    Yesterday, at Bapaume, you saw full well
    How furiously I put to flight the Count
    Of Bucquoi. Like an avalanche I hurled
    My men on his: thrice and again I charged.

CYRANO *(without lifting his face from his book).*
    And your white scarf?

DE GUICHE *(surprised and satisfied).*   You know that
    detail too?
    It came about, that as I wheeled my horse,
    Rallying my soldiers for the final charge,
    A pack of fugitives dragged me along
    Close to the enemy's ranks. I was in danger
    Of being taken prisoner and shot;
    When I had wit enough to drop to earth
    The scarf that showed my military rank,
    And so was able to escape the Spaniards
    Without their recognition,—then return,
    Leading my rallied force, and win the fight!
    —What say you of this feat?
(The Cadets appear not to listen; but their cards and dice-boxes remain in the air, the smoke of their pipes in their cheeks. A pause.)

CYRANO.   That Henry Fourth
    Would never have agreed, 'gainst any odds,
    To take one feather from his snow-white crest.
    (Silent joy. The cards fall, the dice drop, the smoke
                    escapes.)
DE GUICHE.   But still the ruse succeeded!
   (Same wait; while games and smoke are suspended.)
CYRANO.   Like enough.
    But it is not an honor lightly yielded,—
    To be a target.
(Cards fall, dice drop, smoke rises, with growing satis-
    faction.)   Now, had I been there
    When the abandoned scarf fell to the ground—
    Our kinds of courage differ, sir, in this—
    I should have picked it up and put it on.
DE GUICHE.   Yes, Gascon boasting still!
CYRANO.   You call it boasting?
    Lend it to me,—and on this very night
    I'll lead the assault, with the scarf draped about me.
DE GUICHE.   Another Gascon offer! You know well
    The scarf was lost within the foemen's lines,
    By the River Scarpe, where, swept by leaden hail,
    No one can go to seek it.
CYRANO *(taking the white scarf from his pocket, and*
    handing it to him).   Here it is!
    (Silence. The Cadets smother their laughter under
  their cards and dice-boxes. De Guiche turns and looks
  at them; they immediately become serious again, and
  begin their games. One of them whistles the mountain
         melody played by the fife.)
DE GUICHE *(taking the scarf).*
    Thanks. With this piece of white I shall be able
    To give a signal—I was loath to give.

(Goes to the rampart, climbs it, and waves the scarf several times in the air.)

ALL. What?

THE SENTINEL *(on top of the rampart)*. See the man down there, who's running hither!

DE GUICHE *(coming down again)*.

He's a pretended spy. He renders us

Great service; for the tidings that he takes

To the enemy are those I give myself;

And so I have a chance to shape their plans.

CYRANO. A scurvy trick!

DE GUICHE *(carelessly tying on his scarf)*.

It works! As we were saying—

Ah, I was about to tell some news. To-night,

Making one effort more to get us food,

The Marshal goes to Dourlens, without drums.

The King's provision-trains are there. He'll join them

By going through the fields; but to get back

With ease, he's taken with him such a force

The foe will have a fair field for attack,

With half the army absent from the camp.

CARBON. Yes, if the Spaniards knew, it would go hard;

But do they know this sally?

DE GUICHE. Yes, they know.

They will attack us.

CARBON. Ah!

DE GUICHE. My false spy came

To warn me of their near assault. He said:

"I can decide for them the very spot.—

At what point do you wish the battle fought?

I'll tell them that it is the least defended,—

And there they'll try their hand."

I answered him:

" 'T is well. Go from the camp. Watch the whole
    line;—

'T will be the spot where I shall give the signal."

CARBON *(to the Cadets).*

Make ready, gentlemen.

(All rise. Noise of swords, and buckling of belts.)

DE GUICHE.   'T is in an hour.

FIRST CADET.   Ah!

(All sit down again, and take up the interrupted game.)

DE GUICHE.   You must gain time. The Marshal will re-
    turn.

CARBON.   And to gain time?

DE GUICHE. You will have the great kindness

    To give your lives!

CYRANO.   Ah,—is this vengeance, then?

DE GUICHE.   I shall make no pretense that, had I loved
    you,

    I should have chosen you for this defense.

    But since none vie with you in reckless daring,

    I serve my King and satisfy my grudge.

CYRANO.   Permit me, sir, to express my gratitude.

DE GUICHE.   I know you like to fight—one to a hun-
    dred!

    You'll not complain that you lack such a task.

                (Goes aside with Carbon.)

CYRANO *(to the Cadets).*

    'T is well! We shall add to the Gascon blazon,

    Which bears six chevrons, sirs—azure and or,

    One chevron more of gules—which still was lacking.

*(De Guiche talks aside with Carbon de Castel-Jaloux,
in the background. Orders are given. The defense is
made ready. Cyrano goes to Christian, who has
remained motionless, his arms crossed.)*

CYRANO *(putting his hand on his shoulder).*
　Christian?
CHRISTIAN *(shaking his head).*　　Roxane!
CYRANO.　Alas!
CHRISTIAN.　At least, I wish
　That I might put my heart's farewell entire
　Into one last sweet letter!
CYRANO.　I had no doubt
　The end would come to-day—
(Takes a letter from his doublet.) And I have made
　Your farewells for you.
CHRISTIAN.　Show it.
CYRANO.　Do you wish?
CHRISTIAN *(taking the letter).*
　Why, yes! *(Opens it, reads and stops.)* Here?
CYRANO.　What?
CHRISTIAN.　This little spot?
CYRANO *(taking the letter quickly and looking at it with
　　an innocent air).*　A spot?
CHRISTIAN.　It is a tear.
CYRANO.　Why, so it is! A poet
　Is caught at his own game. That is the charm!
　You understand—this note, 'tis very moving;
　It made me weep, myself, while writing.
CHRISTIAN.　Weep?
CYRANO.　Why, yes; because—to die is nothing much;
　But—see her ne'er again! Ay, there's the rub!
　For I shall never—*(Christian looks at him.)* We shall
　ne'er—*(Sharply.)* You will.
CHRISTIAN *(snatching the letter from him).*
　Give me this letter.
　　　　(A noise in the distance in the camp.)
VOICE OF A SENTINEL.　Halt there! Who goes there?

(Shots. Sounds of voices. Rattle of bells.)

CARBON.   What is 't?

THE SENTINEL *(on the rampart)*. A carriage.

CRIES.   What, here—in the camp?
   It enters! It seems from the enemy!
   Fire—No! The driver shouts—Shouts what? He shouts:
   "On the King's service!"
   *(Everyone is on the ramparts looking out. The bells
                  approach.)*

DE GUICHE.   What, the King?
                  (They come down and fall in line.)

CARBON.   Hats off!

DE GUICHE *(from the wings)*.
   From the King.—Take your places, wretched rabble!
   That he may enter in befitting state.
*(The carriage enters at full speed,—covered with mud
   and dust, curtains drawn, two grooms behind,—and
                  stops short.)*

CARBON *(shouting)*.
   Beat the assembly! *(Ruffle of drums. All the Cadets
   uncover.)* Lower the step!
          (Two men rush forward, the door opens.)

ROXANE *(jumping from the carriage)*. Good morning!
*(The sound of a woman's voice raises the whole line,
   which was bowing low. Blank amazement.)*

Scene V.

The Same; Roxane.

DE GUICHE. On the King's service! You?

ROXANE.   The sole King, Love!

CYRANO.   Good God!

CHRISTIAN *(rushing forward)*. You! Why?

ROXANE.   This siege was far too long.

CHRISTIAN.   Why?

ROXANE.   I'll tell you.

CYRANO *(who at the sound of her voice has remained motionless, rooted to the spot, without daring to turn his eyes toward her)*.   God! now dare I look at her!

DE GUICHE.   You cannot stay here.

ROXANE *(gaily)*.   Oh, yes—but I can!

   Will you hand me a drum? *(Sits down on a drum which is handed to her.) (She laughs.)* There! Many thanks.

   They fired on my carriage! *(Proudly.)* A patrol!
It looks made of a pumpkin, does it not?
As in the fairy-tale; and the lackeys changed
From rats. *(Throwing a kiss to Christian.)*
Good morning! *(Looking at all of them.)*
You do not look gay.
You know 'tis far to Arras? *(Seeing Cyrano.)*
Cousin, I'm charmed!

CYRANO *(advancing)*.
   But how, Madame?—

ROXANE.   How did I find the army?
Heavens, my friend, 'twas simple: I but went
Where'er I saw the land laid waste. Such horrors!
I should not have believed, had I not seen.
If that, sirs, be the service of your King,
Mine is far better.

CYRANO.   Well, but this is mad.
   Where did you pass, and how did you get through?

ROXANE.   Where? Through the Spanish lines!

FIRST CADET. An evil lot!

DE GUICHE. But how did you contrive to pass their
  lines?

LE BRET. It must have been no easy task.

ROXANE. Why, yes!
  I simply sent my carriage at full speed:
  If a hidalgo showed his lofty air,
  I merely beamed on him my sweetest smile.
  And, as the Spaniards are the most gallant folk
  In the world,—no offense to the French,—I passed.

CARBON. Yes, 'tis a passport sure, that smile of yours.
  But still they often must have asked of you
  Whither you went at such a pace, Madame?

ROXANE. They often did: and then I always answered:
  "I go to see my lover!" Then the Spaniard,
  E'en of the fiercest air, would gravely close
  My carriage door,—and, with a courtly gesture
  The King himself would envy, wave away
  The guns already levelled at my breast;
  And—gorgeous in his grace and in his pride,
  While his spurs clanked beneath his mantle's train,
  And his hat waved its sweeping plumes in air—
  He would bow low, and say: "Pass, Señorita!"

CHRISTIAN. But—

ROXANE. I said, "My lover," yes; but, pardon me,—
  You understand, if I had said, "My husband,"
  None would have let me pass.

CHRISTIAN. But—

ROXANE. What's the matter?

DE GUICHE. You must depart.

ROXANE. I?

CYRANO. Quickly.

LE BRET. Yes, at once!

CHRISTIAN. Yes!

ROXANE. Why?

CHRISTIAN (*embarrassed*). The fact is—

CYRANO (*same tone*). In the next half-hour—

DE GUICHE (*same tone*). About—

CARBON (*same tone*). 'Tis better—

LE BRET (*same tone*). You might—

ROXANE. I shall stay.

A battle's near!

ALL. Oh, no!

ROXANE. This is my husband!
> (*Throws herself in Christian's arms.*)

Let me be slain with him.

CHRISTIAN. What eyes you have!

ROXANE. I'll tell you why.

DE GUICHE (*in despair*). This is a fearful post!

ROXANE (*turning*). What! fearful?

CYRANO. And in proof, he's given it

To us.

ROXANE (*to De Guiche*). Ah! then you wish me widowed?

DE GUICHE. I swear!—

ROXANE. No, I am somewhat mad just now.

I shall not go away—and 'tis amusing.

CYRANO. What! Has Madame become a heroine?

ROXANE. Monsieur de Bergerac, I am your cousin.

A CADET. We will defend you.

ROXANE (*catching the fever more and more*).

Friends, that I believe!

ANOTHER (*in delight*).

The whole camp smells of iris.

ROXANE. I have on

A hat which will look very well in battle.

(*Looking at De Guiche.*)
Perchance 'tis time the Count should go away,—
They might begin!

DE GUICHE.   This is too much! I go
To inspect my cannon, and return at once.
You still have time; pray change your mind.

ROXANE.   No, never!

(*Exit De Guiche.*)

Scene VI.

The Same; without De Guiche.

CHRISTIAN (*pleading*).   Roxane!—

ROXANE.   No!

FIRST CADET (*to the others*).   She will stay.

ALL (*rushing about and jostling each other as they try to make themselves presentable.*)   A comb—A brush—
Some soap—My clothes are torn; give me a needle—
A ribbon—Here, your mirror—Now, my gauntlets!—
Your curling-irons—and a razor,—quick!

ROXANE (*to Cyrano, who still pleads with her*).
No,—naught shall make me stir from out this place!

CARBON (*after having, like the rest, tightened his belt, dusted his clothes, brushed his hat, arranged his plume, and drawn on his gauntlets, advances towards Roxane and with great ceremony*).
Perhaps it would be fitting to present,
Since the affair stands thus, these gentlemen,
Who'll have the honor to die before your eyes.

(*Roxane bows and waits, on Christian's arm, standing. Carbon introduces.*)

Baron de Peyrescous de Colignac.

THE CADET *(bowing).*   Madame!

CARBON *(continuing).*

Baron de Casterac de Cahuzac;

The Vidame de Malgouyre Estressac Lésbas d' Escarabiot;

Chevalier d'Antignac-Juzet;

Baron Hillot de Blagnac-Saléchan de Castel-Crabioules.

ROXANE.   How many names has each of you?

BARON HILLOT.   A string.

CARBON.   Open the hand that holds your kerchief.

ROXANE *(opens her hand and the handkerchief falls).* Why?

(The whole company rushes forward to pick it up.)

CARBON *(picking it up quickly).*

My company had no standard. But, in faith,
The finest in the camp floats o'er it now!

ROXANE *(smiling).*   'T is rather small.

CARBON *(tying the kerchief to the staff of his captain's lance).*   But it is all of lace.

A CADET *(to the others).*

I should die gladly, having seen this vision,
If I had only one small bite to eat.

CARBON *(who had heard him; indignantly).*

Shame,—speak of eating when a lady fair—

ROXANE.   But the camp's air is sharp,—I'm hungry too,—
Pasties, and game, and wines—that is my choice.
Will you be kind enough to bring them?

> *(Consternation.)*

A CADET.   All?

ANOTHER.   Good Lord! Where shall we get them?

ROXANE *(tranquilly).*   In my carriage.

ALL. What!

ROXANE.   But they must be boned, and carved, and
    served.

Look at my coachman closer, gentlemen,

And you will recognize a very genius.

Each sauce shall be served hot, if you prefer.

THE CADETS (*rushing towards the carriage*).

'T is Ragueneau. (*Acclamations.*)

Oh, oh!

ROXANE (*following them with her eyes*).

Poor boys!

CYRANO (*kissing her hand*).   Good fairy!

RAGUENEAU (*standing on the seat like a charlatan in a
    public square*).

Gentlemen—

(*Enthusiasm.*)

THE CADETS.   Bravo! Bravo!

RAGUENEAU.   The Spaniards failed

To see the feast, when the feast of beauty passed.
    (*Applause.*) (*Cyrano talks aside to Christian.*)

RAGUENEAU.   So taken up with gallantry they were

They never saw (*takes from the seat a dish, which he
    lifts up*) the galantine![7]

(*Applause. The galantine is passed from hand to hand.*)

CYRANO (*aside to Christian*).   I beg you,

One word!

RAGUENEAU.   And Venus[8] so filled every eye

That secretly Diana brought away (*brandishes a leg
    of venison*)

The trophies of her hunt.

(*Enthusiasm. The leg is seized by twenty outstretched
    hands.*)

CYRANO (*aside to Christian*).   I must speak with you.

ROXANE *(to the Cadets, who come down, their arms full of provisions).*

Spread this upon the ground. *(Lays a cloth on the grass, aided by the two footmen who were behind the carriage. To Christian.)* Make yourself useful!

(Christian goes to help her. Cyrano makes a restless movement.)

RAGUENEAU. A truffled peacock!

FIRST CADET *(radiantly, coming down while cutting a large slice of ham).*

Thunder! we shall have

One royal gorge at least, before we die—

(quickly catching himself up as he sees Roxane)

—A royal feast, I mean,—I beg your pardon!

RAGUENEAU *(tossing out the cushions of the carriage).*

The cushions are all stuffed with ortolans![9]

(Great tumult. The cushions are ripped up. Laughter and joy.)

THIRD CADET. Ah!

RAGUENEAU *(tossing out bottles of red wine).*

Flasks of rubies! *(of white wine)*

Flasks of topaz, too!

ROXANE *(throwing a folded tablecloth into Cyrano's face).*

Unfold this cloth—catch it—and look alive!

RAGUENEAU *(waving one of the carriage-lamps, which he has wrenched off).*

And every lantern is a little cupboard.

CYRANO *(aside to Christian, while they together arrange the cloth).*

I must speak with you, ere you speak to her.

RAGUENEAU *(more and more rhapsodical).*

Even my whip-handle is a giant sausage!

ROXANE *(pouring wine and serving).*
  Since they will kill us—heavens! let us laugh
  At all the rest. Everything for the Gascons!
  If De Guiche come, let no one bid him sit.
            (Going from one to another.)
  There, you have time enough—don't eat so fast—
  But drink a little!—Why these tears?
FIRST CADET.   'T is too good!—
ROXANE. Tush!—red or white?—Bread for Monsieur de
    Carbon.
  A knife—your plate!— Some champagne? Or a wing?
CYRANO *(who follows her, his arms full of plates, helping
    her wait).*   I love her!
ROXANE *(going towards Christian).*   You?
CHRISTIAN.   No, nothing.
ROXANE.   Yes, this biscuit,
  Dipped in some muscatel,—two fingers only!
CHRISTIAN *(trying to detain her).*
  Oh, tell me why you came!
ROXANE.   My duty now
  Is to these luckless lads. Hush!—in a moment.
LE BRET *(who has gone to the background, to hand up to
    the Sentinel on the rampart a loaf of bread on the
    end of a lance).*
  De Guiche!
CYRANO.   Quick, hide the bottles, plates, and baskets!
  Let us show nothing! *(To Ragueneau.)*
  Get back on your box!
  Is all well hidden?
*(In a twinkling everything is pushed into the tents, or
hidden under their clothes, their cloaks, or their hats.
    De Guiche enters briskly—and stops suddenly,
            sniffing. Silence.)*

Scene VII.

The Same; De Guiche.

DE GUICHE.   That smells good.

A CADET *(humming with a preoccupied air)*.
   To-lo—

DE GUICHE *(stopping and looking at him)*.
   What is the matter with you? You're quite red.

THE CADET.   I? Nothing—'tis my blood.—We'll fight—
   it starts—

ANOTHER.   Poum, poum!

DE GUICHE *(turning)*.   What's that?

THE CADET *(slightly intoxicated)*.   Nothing—a little song!

DE GUICHE. You're gay, my lad.

THE CADET.   'T is the approach of danger.

DE GUICHE *(calling Carbon de Castel-Jaloux to give an
      order)*.   Here, Captain, I— *(Stops, looking at
      him.)* The deuce! you're cheerful too!

CARBON *(blushing scarlet, and hiding a bottle behind his
      back with furtive movement)*.
   Oh!

DE GUICHE.   There is left one cannon I've had brought.
            (Points to a place in the wing.)
   There, in the corner—use it, if you need.

A CADET *(strutting about)*.
   Charming attention!

ANOTHER *(smiling at him graciously)*.
   Kindly thoughtfulness!

DE GUICHE.   Oh! they are mad! *(Drily.)*
   And being quite unused
   To cannon, take good heed to the recoil.

FIRST CADET.   Oh, pfft!

DE GUICHE *(going to him, furious).* But!—

THE CADET. Gascon guns never recoil.

DE GUICHE *(taking him by the arm and shaking him).* You're drunk!—on what?

THE CADET *(superbly).* Upon the smell of powder.

DE GUICHE *(shrugging his shoulders, pushing him away and going quickly to Roxane).* Quick, Madame. What have you resolved to do?

ROXANE. I stay.

DE GUICHE. Flee!

ROXANE. No!

DE GUICHE. Well, since the case stands thus, Give me a musket!

CARBON. What?

DE GUICHE. I also stay.

CYRANO. But, sir, this savors somewhat of bravado.

FIRST CADET. You are a Gascon, then, despite your lace?

DE GUICHE. I do not leave a woman in distress.

SECOND CADET *(to the First).* Really! I think we well might give him food. *(All the provisions reappear as if by magic.)*

DE GUICHE *(his eyes lighting up).* Provisions!

THIRD CADET. Yes, they came from every cloak.

DE GUICHE *(mastering himself, and with dignity).* Do you then think that I will eat your leavings?

CYRANO *(bowing).* You're making progress now.

DE GUICHE *(proudly).* I shall fight fasting.

FIRST CADET *(exulting with delight).* There spoke a Gascon.

DE GUICHE *(smiling).* I?

THE CADET. He's one of us!

(All begin to dance.)

CARBON DE CASTEL-JALOUX *(who has disappeared for a
    moment behind the rampart, reappearing on top).*

I've placed my lancers there, in open order.

(Points out a line of pikes over the top of the rampart.)

DE GUICHE *(to Roxane, bowing).*

  Will you accept my hand for the review?

    *(She takes it, and they go toward the rampart.
      Everyone uncovers, and follows them.)*

CHRISTIAN *(going to Cyrano quickly).*

  Speak quick!

    *(At the moment when Roxane appears on the top of
      the rampart, the lances disappear, lowered
      in the salute; a shout is raised; she bows.)*

THE LANCERS *(without).*   Hurrah! Hurrah!

CHRISTIAN.   What was the secret?

CYRANO.   If perchance Roxane—

CHRISTIAN.   Well!

CYRANO.   Should speak to you

  Of letters—

CHRISTIAN.   Oh, I know!—

CYRANO.   Have not the folly

  To show surprise.

CHRISTIAN.   At what?

CYRANO.   Well, I must tell you—

  Oh, Lord! 'twas simple, as I see to-day,

  When I see her. You have—

CHRISTIAN.   Speak quick!

CYRANO.   You have

  Written her oftener than you think.

CHRISTIAN.   How's that?

CYRANO.   I took it on myself, and was your spokesman!

  I sometimes wrote, and never let you know.

CHRISTIAN. Ah?

CYRANO. It was simple.

CHRISTIAN.   How did you contrive it?
  Since the blockade—

CYRANO.   Oh, I could pass ere daybreak.

CHRISTIAN (*folding his arms*).
  And that was simple, too? How many times
  A week have I then written—two? three? four?

CYRANO. Oftener.

CHRISTIAN.   Every day?

CYRANO. Yes—twice a day.

CHRISTIAN (*violently*).
  And that made you so drunk with sheer delight
  That you braved death—

CYRANO (*seeing Roxane returning*).   Hush! Hush! Not
    before her!
        (*Quickly goes back into his tent.*)

Scene VIII.

Roxane. Christian in the background. Cadets coming
  and going. Carbon and De Guiche give orders.

ROXANE (*running to Christian*).
  And now, Christian!—

CHRISTIAN (*taking her hands*).   And now; now tell me why,
  By frightful roads, through this rough soldiery,
  You came to join me here?

ROXANE.   It was your letters!

CHRISTIAN.   What?

ROXANE.   The worse for you, if I have risked these
    dangers.

Your letters turned my head. Ah, think how many
You've written me this month; and every one
Was better than the last!

CHRISTIAN.   What, for a few
Little love-letters—

ROXANE.   Hush, you cannot know!
'T is true I've worshipped you since on that evening,
Beneath my window—with a voice whose tones
I had not heard before—your soul began
To make itself known to me. Well, your letters,
You see, for this past month, have been the same
As listening to your voice the livelong day,—
Your voice, as 'twas that evening, soft and tender—
Like a caress. The worse for you, I came!
For had Ulysses written words like yours
Penelope would ne'er have stayed at home
And plied her spinning-wheel; but mad like Helen
She would have sent her fleeces all a-packing,
And gone to seek her husband.

CHRISTIAN.   But—

ROXANE.   I read—
I read again. I felt myself grow faint.
I was your own; and every little page
Was like a petal flying from your soul.
I felt, in each word of your burning letters,
Your love—strong and sincere.

CHRISTIAN.   Sincere and strong?
You felt it there, Roxane?

ROXANE.   Indeed, I did!

CHRISTIAN.   And you have come?

ROXANE.   Oh, Christian! Oh, my master!
(You'd raise me up if I should cast myself
Down at your knees! But 'tis my soul I cast;

And you will ne'er be able to raise that up.)
I come to crave your pardon. 'T is the hour
To pray for pardon—since death stands close at hand—
For having lightly loved you at the first,
Moved only by your comeliness.

CHRISTIAN (*with alarm*).   Roxane!

ROXANE.   Later, dear friend, growing less frivolous,—
A bird that hops before he quite can fly,—
Your soul fast holding what your looks had caught,
I loved you for them both at once!

CHRISTIAN.   And now?

ROXANE.   Now, 'tis yourself that doth outshine yourself;
And for your soul alone I love you now.

CHRISTIAN (*recoiling*).   Roxane!

ROXANE. Be happy, then; since to be loved
For what is but the fleeting moment's dress
Must wring with pain a noble, glowing heart.
But now your well-loved thought is what I see!
The comeliness with which you pleased me first
I see more clearly—yet I see it not.

CHRISTIAN.   Oh!

ROXANE.   You have doubts of such a victory?

CHRISTIAN (*sadly*).   Roxane!

ROXANE.   I know you cannot yet believe
This love of mine—

CHRISTIAN.   I care not for this love!
I would be loved more simply, for—

ROXANE.   For what
Women have loved in you until this hour?
Now let yourself be loved in nobler fashion!

CHRISTIAN.   No. Better as it was!

ROXANE.   You do not see!
'Tis now that I love more,—that I love most,

'Tis what makes you yourself that I adore;—
And even less fair—

CHRISTIAN.   Hush!

ROXANE.   I'd love you still.
If you should lose all comeliness at once—

CHRISTIAN.   Oh, say not so!

ROXANE.   'T is what I mean!

CHRISTIAN.   What! ugly?

ROXANE.   Ugly. I swear it!

CHRISTIAN.   God!

ROXANE.   Your joy is deep?

CHRISTIAN *(with smothered voice)*.   Yes.

ROXANE.   What's the matter?

CHRISTIAN *(pushing her away gently)*. Nothing,—a
    word,—a moment.

ROXANE. But—

CHRISTIAN *(pointing out a group of Cadets in the back-
    ground)*.
    From these poor lads my love takes you away!
    Go,—smile on them a little, ere they die—

ROXANE *(much moved)*. Dear Christian!
    *(Goes toward the Gascons, who crowd respectfully
        around her.)*

Scene IX.

Christian. Cyrano in the background. Roxane talking
    with Carbon and some Cadets.

CHRISTIAN *(calling toward Cyrano's tent)*.
    Cyrano!

CYRANO *(reappearing, armed for battle)*.
    What? You are pale!

CHRISTIAN.   No longer does she love me!

CYRANO.   What?

CHRISTIAN.   'T is you.

CYRANO.   No!

CHRISTIAN.   'T is my soul she loves.

CYRANO.   No.

CHRISTIAN.   Yes, 'tis so.
    'T is really you she loves;—you love her, too!

CYRANO.   I?

CHRISTIAN.   I know it!

CYRANO.   It is true!

CHRISTIAN.   Madly!

CYRANO.   Yes, more!

CHRISTIAN.   Tell her.

CYRANO.   No!

CHRISTIAN.   Why not?

CYRANO.   Why? Look at my face!

CHRISTIAN.   She'd love me—ugly.

CYRANO.   Did she tell you so?

CHRISTIAN.   She did.

CYRANO.   Ah, I am glad she told you that!
    But stop,—do not believe this foolish thing.
    God! I am glad she even had the thought
    To say so! Do not take her at her word.
    Become not ugly;—she'd bear me a grudge!

CHRISTIAN.   That's what I wish to see.

CYRANO.   No!

CHRISTIAN.   Let her choose!
    For you shall tell her all.

CYRANO.   No, not this torture!

CHRISTIAN.   Shall I then kill your joy,—since I am fair?
    'T is too unjust!

CYRANO.   And shall I bury yours?—

Because, thanks to the hazard of my birth,
I have the gift of putting into words
That which perchance you feel?

CHRISTIAN.   Yes, tell her all.

CYRANO.   He will insist on tempting me! 'T is sad.

CHRISTIAN.   I'm weary of this rival in myself.

CYRANO.   Christian!

CHRISTIAN.   Our union—secret, all unknown—
May break, if we survive!

CYRANO.   He still insists!—

CHRISTIAN.   I must be loved myself, or not at all!
I go to see what is on foot—I go
To the end of our lines; then I return.
Speak; let her choose between us.

CYRANO.   'T will be you.

CHRISTIAN.   But—that I hope. *(Calls.)* Roxane!

CYRANO.   No! No!

ROXANE *(running up).*   What is it?

CHRISTIAN.   Cyrano has important news to tell.
(She goes quickly to Cyrano. Christian goes out.)

Scene X.

Roxane, Cyrano; then Le Bret, Carbon de Castel-
Jaloux, the Cadets, Ragueneau, De Guiche, etc.

ROXANE.   Something important?—

CYRANO *(in desperation).*
He has gone—'Twas nothing.
He makes much out of little. You should know him
Better by this time.

ROXANE *(quickly).* He did not believe

What I just said. I saw he had his doubts.

CYRANO *(taking her hand)*.

But did you, then, tell him the very truth?

ROXANE. Yes, I should love him, e'en *(hesitates a second)*—

CYRANO *(smiling sadly)*. It troubles you

To say the word before me?

ROXANE. But—

CYRANO. 'Twill not

Hurt me.—E'en ugly?

ROXANE. Yes. *(Musketry without.)* Ah, there's a shot!

CYRANO. Hideous?

ROXANE. Hideous!

CYRANO. Disfigured?

ROXANE. Yes.

CYRANO. Grotesque?

ROXANE. But naught could make him that to me!

CYRANO. You still would love him?

ROXANE. Yes, and even more!

CYRANO *(losing his head. Aside)*.

My God,—perhaps 'tis true; and bliss at last!

(To Roxane.)

I—Roxane, listen—

LE BRET *(entering rapidly, calls in a low voice)*. Cyrano!

CYRANO *(turning)*. What?

LE BRET. Hush!

(Speaks to him inaudibly.)

CYRANO *(dropping Roxane's hand with a cry)*. Ah!

ROXANE. What's the matter?

CYRANO *(to himself in stupefaction)*. It is done.

ROXANE. What now! They fire?

(Climbs up to look out.)

CYRANO. 'Tis done. I ne'er can tell you now.

ROXANE (*wishing to rush forward*).
> What's going on?

CYRANO (*quickly stopping her*).   Nothing!
> (*Some Cadets enter, concealing something which they
> are carrying; and forming a group, they prevent
> Roxane from approaching.*)

ROXANE.   These men!

CYRANO (*drawing her away*).   Let be—
> I was about to tell you? Nothing, nothing!
> I swear it, Madame. (*Solemnly.*) I swear that Christian's spirit
> And Christian's soul were—(*stopping himself in
> alarm*)—are the greatest—

ROXANE.   Were?
> (*With a great cry.*) Oh! (*Rushes forward and scatters
> every one.*)

CYRANO.   It is done!

ROXANE (*seeing Christian wrapped in his cloak*).
> Christian!

LE BRET (*to Cyrano*).   The foe's first fire!
> (*Roxane throws herself on Christian's body. More
> firing. Rattling of arms. Drums.*)

CARBON (*sword in hand*).
> 'Tis the attack! To arms!
> (*Followed by the Cadets, he goes to the other side of
> the rampart.*)

ROXANE.   Christian!

CARBON'S VOICE (*behind the rampart*).
> Make haste.

ROXANE.   Christian!

CARBON.   *Fall in!*

ROXANE.   Christian!

CARBON.   *Measure—fuses!*

(Ragueneau runs up, with water in a helmet.)

CHRISTIAN *(with dying voice).*   Roxane!

CYRANO *(quick and aside in Christian's ear; while Roxane distractedly dips into the water a piece of linen torn from her breast to bathe his wounds).*

I have told all. She loves thee still.
                         (Christian closes his eyes.)

ROXANE.   What is't, my love?

CARBON.   *Draw ramrods!*

ROXANE *(to Cyrano).*   Is he dead?

CARBON.   *Bite charges! Ready! Load!*

ROXANE.   I feel his cheek
Grow cold against my own.

CARBON.   *Take aim!*

ROXANE.   A letter
Upon him! *(Opens it.)*   'Tis for me.

CYRANO *(aside).*   My letter!

CARBON.   *Fire.*
                    (Musketry, shouts, noise of battle.)

CYRANO *(trying to disengage his hand; which Roxane holds, kneeling).*

Roxane, the fight is on!

ROXANE *(holding him back).*

Stay yet a while.

He's dead. You were the only one who knew him.
                         (Weeps softly.)

—Was he not wonderful?—a chosen being?

CYRANO *(standing bareheaded).*

Yes, Roxane.

ROXANE.   And a poet to adore?

CYRANO.   Yes, Roxane.

ROXANE.   And a lofty spirit?

CYRANO.   Yes.

ROXANE.   A mighty heart, undreamt of by the crowd,—
    A glorious soul and charming?

CYRANO (*stoutly*).   Yes, Roxane!

ROXANE (*throwing herself on Christian's body*).   He's
    dead!

CYRANO (*aside, drawing his sword*).   And only death is
    left for me—
    Since she mourns me in him, and knows it not.
                    (*Trumpets in the distance.*)

DE GUICHE (*reappearing on the rampart, helmet off,
        wounded in the forehead; with thundering voice*).
    The promised signal! Hear the blaring brass!
    The French will quickly reach the camp with food!
    Hold hard a moment longer.

ROXANE.   On his letter
    Are blood and tears!

A VOICE WITHOUT (*shouting*).   Surrender!

CADETS' VOICES.   No!

RAGUENEAU (*perched on his carriage, watching the bat-
        tle over the rampart*).   The danger
    Grows greater.

CYRANO (*to De Guiche, pointing out Roxane*).
    Take her hence. I'll join the charge.

ROXANE (*kissing the letter, with dying voice*).
    His blood! His tears!

RAGUENEAU (*leaping from the carriage to run towards
        her*).   She's fainted!

DE GUICHE (on *the rampart, to the Cadets, in fury*).
    Hold your ground!

A VOICE (*without*).   Lower your arms!

CADETS' VOICES.   No!

CYRANO (*to De Guiche*).   You have fairly proved

Your courage, sir, already. (*Pointing to Roxane.*)
Flee, and save her!

DE GUICHE (*runs to Roxane, and carries her away in his arms*).

So be it! But we still may win the day
If you gain time

CYRANO. 'T is well! (*Calling to Roxane, whom De Guiche, with Ragueneau's help, carries off in a faint.*)   Farewell, Roxane!

(*Confusion; shouts. Cadets reappear, wounded, and fall upon the stage. Cyrano, rushing into the battle, is stopped on top of the rampart by Carbon, covered with blood.*)

CARBON. Our line is broken! I have had two wounds!

CYRANO (*shouting to the Gascons*).

Stand fast! Hold hard, my lads! (*To Carbon, whom he holds up.*)   Be not afraid.

Two deaths I must avenge: my friend,—my joy!

(*They descend. Cyrano brandishes the lance on which is fastened Roxane's kerchief.*)

Float, little flag of lace that bears her name.

(*Plants it in the ground, and shouts to the Cadets.*)

Fall on them! Crush them down! (*To the fifer*). And blow your fife.

(*The fifer plays. The wounded raise themselves. Cadets, climbing up the rampart, rally around Cyrano and the little flag. The carriage, transformed into a redoubt, is covered and filled with men, and bristles with arquebuses.*)

A CADET (*appearing on top of the rampart, in retreat, but still fighting, shouts.*)

They scale the rampart.

(Falls dead.)

CYRANO.   Give them a salute.

(The rampart is crowded in a moment with a terrible array of the enemy. The great Imperial standards appear.)

CYRANO.   Fire!

(General volley.)

A SHOUT IN THE ENEMY'S RANKS.   Fire!

(Murderous reply. The Cadets fall on every side.)

A SPANISH OFFICER *(uncovering).*   Who are these, who all court death!

CYRANO *(reciting, erect in the midst of the bullets.)*

> These be Cadets of Gascony,—
> Carbon de Castel-Jaloux's men:
> They fight, they lie full shamelessly,—

(darts forward, followed by a few survivors)

> —These be Cadets—

(The rest is lost in the battle.)

CURTAIN.

FIFTH ACT

Cyrano's Gazette.

Fifteen years after, in 1655. The park of the convent oc-cupied by the Sisters of the Cross, at Paris. Superb foliage. To the left, the house; a great terrace upon which several doors open. An enormous tree in the centre of the stage, standing alone in the middle of a little oval opening. To the right, in the foreground,

among boxwood bushes, a semicircular stone bench.
The rear of the stage is crossed by an avenue of chest-
nuts; which leads on the right (in the background) to
the door of a chapel, half seen through the branches.
Through the double curtain of trees formed by this
avenue are seen stretches of lawn, other avenues,
small groves; the perspective of the park; the sky. A
little side door of the chapel opens on a colonnade,
garlanded with reddened vines, the colonnade disap-
pearing on the right in the foreground, behind the
box. It is autumn. The foliage shows yellow above the
green lawns. Dark spots of box and yew trees, still
green. A circle of dead leaves under each tree. The
leaves are scattered over the whole stage, crackle
under foot in the avenues, and half cover the terrace
and the benches. Between the bench on the right and
the tree stands a large embroidery-table, in front of
which a low chair has been placed. Baskets full of
skeins and worsteds. A piece of embroidery already
begun. When the curtain rises, Sisters are coming
and going in the park; some are seated on the bench
around an older nun. The leaves are falling.

Scene I.

Mother Margaret, Sister Martha, Sister Claire; Other
  Sisters.

SISTER MARTHA (to Mother Margaret).
  Sister Claire glanced i' the mirror twice, to see
  How sat her headdress.

MOTHER MARGARET (*to Sister Claire*).   It is very ugly.

SISTER CLAIRE.   But I saw Sister Martha steal a plum,
This morning, from the tart.

MOTHER MARGARET (*to Sister Martha*).   A naughty deed!

SISTER CLAIRE.   But such a little look!

SISTER MARTHA.   So small a plum!

MOTHER MARGARET.   I'll tell Monsieur Cyrano all, to-
night.

SISTER CLAIRE (*alarmed*).
No, he will mock us.

SISTER MARTHA.   He will call the nuns
Very coquettish—

SISTER CLAIRE.   Very fond of sweets—

MOTHER MARGARET (*smiling*).
And very good.

SISTER CLAIRE.   But, mother, is't not so,—
He's come each Saturday these ten years past?

MOTHER MARGARET.   Yes, longer! Ever since his cousin
joined
Her worldly mourning to our linen robes,
And sought for peace with us,—fourteen years since;
Like some great black-plumed bird 'mid our white
flock.

SISTER MARTHA.   He only, since she first took refuge here,
Can charm away her never-lessening grief.

ALL THE SISTERS.   He is so merry—'T is cheerful when
he comes—
He teases us—He's kind—We like him well—
We must prepare for him our choicest sweets—

SISTER MARTHA.   But yet he is not a good Catholic!

SISTER CLAIRE.   We shall convert him.

THE SISTERS.   Yes, yes!

MOTHER MARGARET.   I forbid!

That is a task you must not undertake.

Trouble him not. He might come less, perchance.

SISTER MARTHA.   But—God—

MOTHER MARGARET.   Be not disturbed! God knows
him well!

SISTER MARTHA.   Yet every Saturday he proudly tells
me,

When he comes in, "I feasted yesterday!"

MOTHER MARGARET.   He tells you that!—The last time
that he came,

Food had not passed his lips for two whole days.

SISTER MARTHA.   Mother!

MOTHER MARGARET.   He's poor.

SISTER MARTHA.   Who told you?

MOTHER MARGARET.   Monsieur le Bret.

SISTER MARTHA.   He gets no help?

MOTHER MARGARET.   No, that would anger him.

*(In an avenue in the background Roxane appears,
dressed in black, with a widow's cap and long veil; De
Guiche, very elegant, but growing old, walks near her.
    They approach slowly. Mother Margaret rises.)*

We must retire—Madame Madeleine

Is walking with a stranger in the park.

SISTER MARTHA *(aside to Sister Claire)*.   The Duc de
Grammont?

SISTER CLAIRE *(looking)*.   Yes, I think it is.

SISTER MARTHA.   He has not come to see her for these
months.

THE SISTERS.   He's busy—with the Court—the Field—

SISTER CLAIRE.   The World!

*(They go out. De Guiche and Roxane come down in
silence, and stop near the embroidery-table.
                    An interval.)*

Scene II.

Roxane, the Duc de Grammont (formerly Comte De
   Guiche); then Le Bret, and Ragueneau.

THE DUKE.   And you will stay here ever—vainly fair,
   And always mourning?
ROXANE.   Always!
THE DUKE.   Faithful still?
ROXANE.   Still faithful.
THE DUKE *(after an interval).*   And you have forgiven me?
ROXANE.   Since I am here.
THE DUKE.   He was a noble soul.
ROXANE.   You should have known him.
THE DUKE.   Ah?   Perhaps I should.
   Perhaps I never knew him well enough.
   Do you still wear his letter next your heart?
ROXANE.   Like some dear relic, on this velvet band.
THE DUKE.   You love him, e'en in death?
ROXANE.   Sometimes it seems
   He is not wholly dead,—our hearts still meet,
   His living love hovers about me still.
THE DUKE *(after another silence).*
   Cyrano comes to see you?
ROXANE.   Often, yes.
   He is for me a journal—this old friend,—
   He comes at such a time. His chair is placed
   Under this tree, whene'er the weather's fine.
   I ply my needle, and I wait for him.
   The clock strikes: and at the last stroke I hear—
   For I no longer even turn my head—
   His stick upon the steps. He seats himself;
   He jests at my eternal needlework;

He tells me the week's doings. (*Le Bret appears on the steps.*)   Oh, Le Bret!
             (*Le Bret descends.*)
How is our friend ?

LE BRET.   Ill!

THE DUKE.   Oh!

ROXANE (*to the Duke*).   He tells it large.

LE BRET.   'T is all as I foretold. Alone and wretched—
His letters ever winning him new foes—
He levels his attacks at every sham:
Sham nobles,—hypocrites,—sham heroes,—wit
Stolen from others;—in short, at all the world.

ROXANE.   But his sword still inspires a mighty dread;
No one will get the best of him.

THE DUKE (*shaking his head*).   Who knows?

LE BRET.   But what I fear is not fair, open fight.
'T is solitude and hunger—winter cold,
Ent'ring his humble room with wolf-like tread,—
Such are the murderers who'll be his death.
—For every day he tighter draws his belt;
His nose is like some piece of antique ivory;
He has one single coat, of wretched black.

THE DUKE.   Oh, he's no upstart rich! It is as well!
Waste not your pity on him!

LE BRET (*with a bitter smile*).   But, my Lord!

THE DUKE.   Waste not your pity on him; he has lived
Without concessions, free in thought and deed.

LE BRET (*as before*).   Your Grace—

THE DUKE (*haughtily*).   I know I've all things; he has naught,—
But I would gladly grasp him by the hand.
(*Bowing to Roxane*). Adieu!

ROXANE.   I will attend you.

*(The Duke bows to Le Bret, and turns toward
the steps with Roxane.)*

THE DUKE *(stopping while she ascends).*
    Yes, sometimes
    I envy him. You see, when all one's life
    Has brought too much success, too lightly won,
    He feels—though he has done no downright wrong—
    A thousand petty quarrels with himself,
    Which all combined together only make
    A dull disgust with life—yet not remorse;
    And while one mounts the steps of worldly state,
    Even the ermine mantle of a duke
    Drags after it a host of vain regrets
    And dead illusions; even as your gown—
    While you mount slowly upward to these doors—
    Drags after it the rustling fallen leaves.

ROXANE *(ironically).* Are you a dreamer?

THE DUKE. Yes! *(Just as he is going out, quickly.)* Monsieur Le Bret!

               (To Roxane.)

    By your leave? A word.
      (Approaches Le Bret and in an undertone.)
    'T is true, no one would dare
    Attack your friend,—but many hate him well:
    And yesterday they told me, at the Queen's,
    "This Cyrano might die by some mishap!"

LE BRET. Ah?

THE DUKE. Let him go out seldom, and be cautious.

LE BRET *(lifting his arms toward heaven).*
    Cautious! He's coming. I shall warn him—But!

ROXANE *(who has remained on the steps, to a sister who
    advances towards her).* What?

THE SISTER. Ragueneau would see you, Madame.

ROXANE.   Bid him enter.
                    (To the Duke and Le Bret.)
   He comes to tell his woes. Having set out
   To be an author, he has been in turn
   Singer—
LE BRET.   Bath-keeper—
ROXANE.   Actor—
LE BRET.   Beadle—
ROXANE.   Barber—
LE BRET.   Lute-player—
ROXANE.   And what will he be to-day?
RAGUENEAU *(entering hurriedly.)*
   Ah, Madame! *(Sees Le Bret.)*   Sir!
ROXANE *(smiling).*   Now you can tell your troubles
   To Le Bret; I'll return.
RAGUENEAU.   But, Madame—
(Roxane goes out, without hearing him, with the Duke.
         He goes down again to Le Bret.)

Scene III.

Le Bret, Ragueneau.

RAGUENEAU.   Well,
   Since you are here, 'tis best she should not know—
   As I was on my way to see your friend,
   And still some twenty paces from his door,
   I saw him coming out. I went to meet him,
   And as he turned the corner of the street,
   From out a window, under which he passed,
   A lackey dropped a stave—By chance? Perhaps!
LE BRET.   The cowards—Cyrano!

RAGUENEAU. I came and saw—

LE BRET. Frightful!

RAGUENEAU. Our friend, Monsieur,—our noble poet,
There on the ground, a great wound in his head.

LE BRET. He's dead?

RAGUENEAU. No, but—Good God! I bore him
Up to his room. His room! Oh, you should see
His wretched pallet!

LE BRET. He is suffering?

RAGUENEAU. No, sir, he is unconscious.

LE BRET. A physician?

RAGUENEAU. One came by courtesy.

LE BRET. Poor Cyrano !
We must not tell this all at once to Roxane.
What did the doctor say?

RAGUENEAU. I hardly know.
He talked of fever; he spoke of the brain—
Oh, you should see him—his poor bandaged head!
Come quickly, there is no one at his side;
And if he rises, sir, he's like to die.

LE BRET (*drawing him toward the right*).
This way, 'tis shorter—through the chapel—come!

ROXANE (*appearing on the steps, and seeing Le Bret departing by the colonnade leading to the little door of the chapel*).
Monsieur Le Bret! (*Le Bret and Ragueneau escape without answering.*) He goes when he is called!
'T is some new history of poor Ragueneau's.
(*Descends the steps.*)

Scene IV.

Roxane, alone; then, for a moment, two Sisters.

ROXANE.   This last September day is very fair.
  My sadness smiles,—in April wrapt in gloom,
  But of a brighter hue when autumn comes.
(Seats herself at her work. Two Sisters come out of the house, and carry a large arm-chair under the tree.)
  Here's the historic chair where my old friend
  Will take his seat.
SISTER MARTHA.   It is the best we have.
ROXANE.   I thank you, Sister. *(The Sisters withdraw.)*
    He will come. *(Takes her seat. The clock strikes.)*
    The clock
  Is striking—my embroid'ry—It has struck.
  I am amazed. Will he for once be late?
  The Sister at the gate—Where is my thimble?
  —Must be exhorting him to penitence.
  I've found it now—*(An interval.)* She is exhorting him.
  He cannot tarry long—A fallen leaf!
(With her finger she brushes away a leaf that has fallen on her work.)
  Besides, nothing could keep him—Now, my scissors?
  Here in my bag.
A SISTER *(appearing on the steps).*   Monsieur de Bergerac.

Scene V.

Roxane, Cyrano; and, a moment later, Sister Martha.

ROXANE *(without turning).*
  What was I saying?

(She sews. Cyrano appears, very pale, with his hat
pulled down over his eyes. A Sister ushers him in and
retires. He starts to walk slowly down the steps,
making a visible effort to hold himself erect, and
leaning on his stick. Roxane works at her embroidery.)
Ah, these faded shades!
Into what pattern shall I fashion them?
      (To Cyrano, in tones of friendly scolding.)
Late—for the first time in full fourteen years!

CYRANO *(reaching the arm-chair, and sitting down;*
      speaking with a cheerful voice, in contrast to his
      expression).

Yes, 'tis absurd, I am beside myself.
I was detained.

ROXANE.   By what?

CYRANO.   Oh, by a most
Untimely visitation!

ROXANE.   By a man
Seeking to fill your ears with petty plaints?

CYRANO.   No, 'twas a woman of the same ill sort.

ROXANE.   You bade her go?

CYRANO.   Yes. "This is Saturday,"
I said: "a day when surely, rain or shine,
I must betake me to a certain house
And pay a visit there. So come again
Within an hour."

ROXANE *(lightly)*. Well, this friend of yours
Will have to wait for you a longer time—
I shall not let you go till evening falls.

CYRANO.   But I may be constrained to go away
A little sooner.
      (He closes his eyes, and is silent for a moment.
      Sister Martha crosses the park, from the chapel

to the steps. Roxane sees her, and signals to her
with a little nod of her head.

ROXANE *(to Cyrano).*   Oh! You will not tease
  Poor Sister Martha?

CYRANO *(smartly, opening his eyes).*   Yes, I think I shall
(With a big, comical voice.) Sister, come here!
(The Sister glides towards him.)   Ha, ha! You carry still
  Your bright eyes always lowered!

SISTER MARTHA *(lifting her eyes with a smile.)*   But—
    (sees his appearance, and makes a movement of
    surprise) Oh!

CYRANO *(aside, indicating Roxane).* Hush!
  'T is nothing. *(In a voice of burlesque boasting.)*
  Yesterday I made a feast!

SISTER MARTHA.   I understand. *(Aside.)* That's why he
  is so pale.
                (In a quick aside to Cyrano.)
  Come to the dining-hall, and you shall take
  A fine great bowl of broth. You will come, now?

CYRANO.   Yes, yes; of course.

SISTER MARTHA.   Now, I am glad to see
  That for this once you can be reasonable.

ROXANE *(hearing them whispering).*
  She's trying to convert you?

SISTER MARTHA.   No, not I!

CYRANO.   Yes, that is true! And yet the pious words
  Fall from your lips in such a plenteous flow
  I am amazed you do not preach to me.
                (With mock anger.)
  Thunder and Mars! I shall amaze you, too,
  For I shall suffer you this very night—
    (pretends to be looking for a subject of raillery
                and to find it)

—To pray for me at chapel!

ROXANE.   Oh, oh, oh!

CYRANO *(laughing)*.   The Sister's stricken dumb.

SISTER MARTHA *(gently)*.   I waited not
For your permission.
                    (Retires.)

CYRANO *(turning to Roxane, who bends over her work.)*
When shall I see the end
Of this interminable needlework?

ROXANE.   I waited for that jest.
    *(At this moment, a puff of wind starts the leaves
                    falling.)*

CYRANO.   Look at the leaves.

ROXANE *(raising her head, and looking far off through
    the vista)*.

They are Venetian yellow. Watch them fall.

CYRANO.   Yes, watch them well—how gracefully they
    fall!
And in their journey short, from branch to earth,
How they put on a final fleeting charm!
And, although loath to molder on the ground,
They strive to give their fall the grace of flight!

ROXANE.   What, are you sad?

CYRANO *(remembering himself)*.   No, not at all, Rox-
    ane.

ROXANE.   Let the leaves fall, and tell me all the news,—
My journal!

CYRANO.   Here it is.

ROXANE.   Ah!

CYRANO *(growing paler and paler, and struggling
    against his pain)*.
Saturday,
The nineteenth of the month, His Majesty,

Having partaken of too many sweets,
Suffered a touch of fever, and was bled.
His illness was found guilty of high treason;
And now his august pulse is calm again!
At the Queen's ball, on Sunday, there were burned
Wax candles seven hundred sixty-three!
They say our troops beat John of Austria!
Four witches have been hanged! The little dog
Of Madame Athis needed medicine—

ROXANE. Monsieur de Bergerac, will you be still!

CYRANO. Nothing on Monday, but Lygdamire's new
lover;—

ROXANE. Oh!

CYRANO. Tuesday the whole Court went to
Fontainebleau;—

Wednesday De Fiesque had "No" from La Montglat;—

Thursday Mancini is Queen of France—almost!—

Friday La Montglat to De Fiesque said "Yes;"

And on the twenty-sixth, on Saturday—
    (Closes his eyes; his head drops. Silence.)

ROXANE *(surprised at hearing nothing more, turns,
looks at him; and getting up in fright).*

He's fainted? *(Rushes towards him, exclaiming).*
Cyrano!

CYRANO *(opening his eyes; with muffled voice).*
What is it? What?

*(Sees Roxane leaning over him; quickly settles his hat
on his head, and draws back in alarm in his chair.)*
No, no! 'T is nothing, nothing! Let me be!

ROXANE. Yet—

CYRANO. 'T is my wound—from Arras—which at
times—

You know—

ROXANE. Poor friend—

CYRANO. 'T is naught. 'T will pass. (*Smiles, with an effort.*) It has passed!

ROXANE. Each of us has his wound; and I have mine,—
An ancient wound that never heals,—just here.
                (*Lays her hand on her breast.*)
Here!—'neath this letter, with its yellowing folds!
Where still you see commingled blood and tears.
                (*Twilight begins to fall.*)

CYRANO. His letter! Once I think you promised me
That I might some day read it—

ROXANE. Do you wish?—

CYRANO. Yes, 'tis my wish, to-day—

ROXANE (*giving him the little bag which hangs about her neck*). Here—

CYRANO (*taking it*). I may open?

ROXANE. Open and read.
(*She returns to her work, folds it, and arranges her worsteds.*)

CYRANO (*reading*):

     "Farewell, Roxane, my death is very near!"

ROXANE (*stopping in astonishment*). Aloud?

CYRANO.

     "This very night, my best-beloved,
     My soul is heavy with unuttered love;
     And now I die; and never, nevermore,
     Shall my eyes feast on you their yearning gaze!"

ROXANE. But how you read his letter—with what voice!

CYRANO.

> "Drunk with your beauty; kissing as they flit
>   Each little graceful movement that you make;
>   And one familiar gesture still I see—
>   The way you touched your forehead!"

ROXANE.   How you read
  This letter!
                    (Night falls imperceptibly.)
CYRANO.

> "And I fain would cry aloud
>   'Farewell!' "

ROXANE.   You read—
CYRANO.

> "My dearest! Oh, my love!
>   My treasure"—

ROXANE.   With a voice—
CYRANO.

> "My best-beloved"—

ROXANE.   A voice that I have somewhere heard before.
*(Approaches softly, without his noticing it; goes behind
his chair, leans over quietly, and looks at the letter. The
                    darkness deepens.)*
CYRANO.

> "My heart has never left you for a breath;
>   And here, and in the world beyond the grave,
>   I am he whose love for you passed every bound."

ROXANE *(laying her hand on his shoulder).*
  But how can you read now? The night has come.

(He starts, turns; sees her close to him; makes a
startled gesture, lowers his head. A long silence. Then,
after it has become quite dark, she says slowly,
clasping her hands).

And for these fourteen years he's played this part
Of the old friend who comes to cheer me up.

CYRANO.   Roxane!

ROXANE.   'T was you!—

CYRANO.   Ah, no, Roxane; not I!

ROXANE.   I should have guessed it, when he spoke my
name.

CYRANO.   Ah, no! It was not I.

ROXANE.   'T was you.

CYRANO.   I swear—

ROXANE.   At last I see it all—the generous cheat!
You wrote the letters—

CYRANO.   No!

ROXANE.   The dear mad words
Were yours—

CYRANO.   No!

ROXANE.   The voice that night was yours.

CYRANO.   I swear it was not!

ROXANE.   And the soul was yours.

CYRANO.   I loved you not!

ROXANE.   You loved me—

CYRANO.   It was he—

ROXANE.   You loved me!

CYRANO.   No.

ROXANE.   But now you speak more soft.

CYRANO.   No, no; my best-beloved, I loved you not.

ROXANE.   How many things since then have come and
gone!
Why have you held your peace for fourteen years?

Since on this letter, which was naught to him,
These tears were yours?
CYRANO.   But the blood was his!
ROXANE.   Then why to-day should you decide to break
This noble silence?
CYRANO.   Why?
        (*Enter Le Bret and Ragueneau, running.*)

Scene VI.

The Same; Le Bret and Ragueneau.

LE BRET.   What madness! I was sure—There he is!
CYRANO (*smiling and straightening up*).
    Why, yes; of course!
LE BRET.   Madame, he's killed himself
By rising.
ROXANE.   But just now, this weakness—
CYRANO.   True,
    My news was not yet finished: Saturday,
    The twenty-sixth, an hour before he dined,
    Monsieur de Bergerac was foully murdered.
        (*Uncovers. His head is seen to be bandaged.*)
ROXANE.   What says he? Cyrano! Look at his head,
    Wrapped in a bandage! Oh! what have they done
    To you! Why?
CYRANO.   *"By the good sword's thrust,*
    Struck by a hero, fall with point in heart!"—
    Yes, I said that. But Destiny's a mocker.
    And here I am, caught by a coward's trick;
    Struck from behind; felled by a faggot's blow
    Wielded by hireling hands,—indeed 'tis well:
    I shall have failed in all things—e'en in death.

RAGUENEAU. Oh, sir!

CYRANO. What are you doing now, my colleague?

RAGUENEAU. I now am candle-snuffer—for Molière.

CYRANO. Molière?

RAGUENEAU. But I shall surely leave to-morrow!
Yes, I am angry with him. Yesterday
"Scapin" was acted; and I plainly saw
He'd stolen a scene from you—

LE BRET. A scene entire!

RAGUENEAU. The famous—"How the devil came he
there?"[1]

LE BRET. Molière stole it from you!

CYRANO. Tush! He's done well!
The scene went off, I trust, with good effect?

RAGUENEAU (*sobbing*).
Oh, sir, they laughed, they laughed!

CYRANO. Yes, all my life
My part has been to prompt—and be forgot.
> (*To Roxane.*)
Rememberest thou the night when Christian wooed,
Under the balcony?—All my life is there!
While I remained below, hid in the dark,
Others have climbed to kisses and to fame!
'T is just; and on the threshold of my tomb,
I own Molière a genius—Christian fair.

(*At this moment the chapel-bell rings, and the nuns are
seen passing through the avenue in the background,
going to mass.*)

Their bell has sounded; let them go to prayers.

ROXANE (*rising to call for help*).
Come! Sister, Sister!

CYRANO. No, no! Go for no one!
When you return, I shall have gone away.

(The nuns have entered the chapel. The organ plays.)
    Music was all I needed—there it is!

ROXANE.   I love you! Live!

CYRANO.   No, in the fairy-tale
   'T is plainly written that when the humbled Prince
   Had heard the words—"I love you," his disguise
   Of horror fled like snow before the sun:
   But you will see that I remain the same.

ROXANE.   And I have wrought your sorrow—even I!

CYRANO.   You? No, not you! 'T is quite the opposite.
   I ne'er knew woman's kindness. E'en my mother
   Thought me not fair. I never had a sister.
   Then I feared sweethearts with their mocking eyes!
   But, thanks to you, I've had at least a friend;
   And through my life a woman's robe has passed.

LE BRET *(pointing out the moonbeams falling through
   the branches).*
   There comes your other friend to see you.

CYRANO *(smiling at the moon).*   Yes!

ROXANE.   I loved but one—and now I lose him twice.

CYRANO.   Le Bret, I'm going,—up to the shining moon,
   And need devise no engine for this flight!

ROXANE.   What did you say?

CYRANO.   Yes, it is there, on high,
   There am I sent to make my paradise.
   More than one soul I love is exiled there:
   Socrates—Galileo. I'll find them all.

LE BRET *(rebelliously).*
   No, no! 'T is too absurd! 'T is too unjust!
   So great a poet! Such a noble heart!
   To die this way! To die—

CYRANO.   Hear Le Bret scold!

LE BRET *(bursting into tears).*   Dear friend!

CYRANO (*rising, his eyes wandering*).
  "These be Cadets of Gascony"—
  The elemental substance— Yes—the "*hic.*"
LE BRET.   List to his science, even in his ravings.
CYRANO.   Copernicus said—
ROXANE.   Oh!
CYRANO.   "How came he there?
  And how the devil fell he in such plight?"

> *Philosopher, physician,*
> *Poet, swordsman, and musician,*
> *And a traveller through the heavens to the moon!*
> *His sword-point always ready,*
> *His sword-arm always steady,*
> *And a lover to whom love was not a boon!*

> *Here lies Hercule-Savinien de Cyrano de Bergerac;*
> *All things in turn he tried; and all things did he lack!*

But pardon—I must go, I may not wait:
You see the moonbeams come to take me hence!
(*Falls back into his seat. Roxane's tears bring him back
  to realities. He looks at her, and caresses her veil.*)
I would not have you shed one tear the less
For Christian—fair and noble. All I ask
Is, when my body shall lie cold in death,
You give a double meaning to these weeds—
And let his mourning be my mourning too!
ROXANE.   I swear it!
CYRANO (*shaken with a great tremor, rises quickly.*)
    No, not there! Not in a chair!
            (*They rush towards him.*)
  Let no one hold me up. (*Leans against the tree.*)
    Only the tree—(*Silence.*)

He comes! I feel already shod with stone,
And gloved with lead. (*Stiffens himself.*) But since
  he's on the way,
I'll meet him standing upright—(*draws his sword*)—
  sword in hand—

LE BRET.   Cyrano!
ROXANE (*fainting*).   Cyrano!
          (*All draw back in terror.*)
CYRANO.   He sees my nose!
Well! Let the flat-nose look me in the face!
          (*Raises his sword.*)
You say 'tis useless? That I know full well!
But I have never fought with hope to win.
No,—it is finer when 'tis all in vain.
Now, who are these—a thousand thronged about me?
I know you well—You are all ancient foes:
Falsehood! (*Strikes with his sword in the air.*) There,
  there! Ha, ha! And Compromise!
Bigotry! Cowardice! (*Strikes.*) Shall I make terms?
No, never! never! There is Folly, too!
I knew that in the end you'd lay me low.
No matter. Let me fight! and fight! and fight!
(*Swings his sword in circles, and stops, panting.*)
You snatch them all away—laurel and rose!
Snatch on! One thing is left in spite of you,
Which I take with me: and this very night,
When I shall cross the threshold of God's house,
And enter, bowing low, this I shall take
Despite you, without wrinkle, without spot—
          (*Rushes forward with brandished sword.*)
And that is—
(*The sword falls from his hands. He staggers, and falls
    into the arms of Le Bret and Ragueneau.*)

ROXANE (*leaning over him, and kissing his forehead*).
  What?
CYRANO (*opens his eyes, recognizes her, and says with a
  smile*).   My stainless soldier's crest!

CURTAIN.

NOTES

First Act

1. **Marquises:** Noblemen of hereditary rank.
2. **Musketeer:** A soldier armed with a musket, which is a light gun with a long barrel that is fired from the shoulder.
3. **Blue-stocking:** A slightly derogatory term used to describe intellectual or literary women. *Blue stockings* referred to the informal dress favored by men who attended London's literary assemblies in the mid-eighteenth century. Women who attended these assemblies became known as *bluestocking ladies* or *bluestockingers*.
4. **Hôtel de Bourgogne:** The first theater in Paris, the Hôtel de Bourgogne was built in 1548 by the Confraternity of the Passion, the Paris actors' monopoly. Its prominence in Parisian theater was not challenged until 1634, when a new theater company was established at the Théâtre du Marais. In 1680,

the two companies merged to form the Comédie-Française.

5. *parterre:* The portion of the ground floor of an auditorium in the rear and on the sides, especially the part just below the balcony.

6. *La Clorise:* A famous pastoral play by Balthazar Baro, which had its premiere at the Hôtel de Bourgogne.

7. **Lackeys:** Footmen or manservants.

8. **Foil:** Light fencing sword without cutting edges and with a button on its point.

9. **A drinker should drink his Burgundy at the Hôtel de Bourgogne:** The hotel is named for the Bourgogne region of France, called Burgundy in English. Burgundy's most famous export is its fine red burgundy wine.

10. **Rotrou . . . and Corneille:** Jean de Rotrou (1609–50) and Pierre Corneille (1606–84) were contemporaries, friends, and rivals: both were among the *cinq auteurs,* five playwrights officially commissioned by Cardinal Richelieu. Corneille is best known for writing *Le Cid* (1637), as well as the tragedy *Horace* (1640) and the comedy *Le Menteur* (1643); Rotrou's most famous plays include *Saint-Genest* (1646) and *Venceslas* (1647).

11. **blow-gun:** A primitive weapon consisting of a long tube through which projectiles are propelled by force of breath.

12. **I sat there:** Although *La Clorise* premiered in 1631, Rostand sets the action in 1640, to coincide with the historical siege of Arras.

13. **Montfleury . . . Bellerose, L'Épy, Beaupré, and Jodelet:** Famous actors at the Hôtel de Bourgogne.

Montfleury was known not only for his acting talents, but his extremely large girth and impassioned style.

14. **Mesdames de Guémenée, Bois Dauphin . . . De Chavigny . . . Boudu, Boissat, Cureau, Porchères, Colomby, Bourzeys, and Bourdon:** Notable ladies of the Louis XIII period.

15. **Barthénoïde, Urimédonte, Félixe, Cassandacë:** Literary ladies, or bluestockings, of the era.

16. **D'Assoucy:** Charles Coypeau d'Assoucy was a friend of Cyrano de Bergerac's and Molière's, and, like the historical Cyrano, also a burlesque author.

17. **muscatel:** A wine made from the muscat grape.

18. **triolet:** Originating in mid-seventeenth-century France, a triolet is a poem of eight lines, typically eight syllables each, which is structured so that the first line recurs as the fourth and seventh lines, and the second line recurs as the eighth.

19. **Gascony:** A region and former province in southwestern France, in the northern foothills of the Pyrenees mountains. Gascony was a major battleground in the Hundred Years' War (1337–1453) and was completely recovered by France in 1453. The Gascons were famous fighters and mountain mercenaries. Their hot-blooded nature and willingness to battle for honor and glory was immortalized by Alexandre Dumas in *The Three Musketeers* (1844).

20. **You know the way!:** Lignière explains to Christian that the Comte de Guiche wishes to arrange a marriage between Roxane and Monsieur de Valvert, an old and dull man. Since de Guiche is so powerful, de Valvert will naturally be "obliging," and de Guiche may have Roxane as his mistress.

21. **Still a Gascon:** As the Gascons have their own region, true to his nationalist French/Gascon spirit, de Guiche has amassed his own court.

22. **The Spaniard will fare very ill in Flanders:** In 1659, under the terms of the Treaty of the Pyrenees, Spain was obliged to cede to France the frontier fortresses in Flanders and Artois.

23. **Porte de Nesle:** In Paris, on the left bank of the river Seine, the Porte de Nesle was a gate next to a defense tower built around 1220 by Philippe Hamelin. Simon de Clermont, the Lord of Nesle, later built a palace next to the tower and gate.

24. **The Cardinal!:** Cardinal Richelieu, chief minister of Louis XIII, was an active patron of the arts and especially the theater. The "latticed box" is his seat in a theater box.

25. **Zephyrus:** In Greek mythology, the west wind.

26. **bantling:** A young child; a brat.

27. **seneschal:** Historically, the chief steward overseeing the domestic affairs of a great medieval house.

28. **Thespis:** Greek dramatic poet (c. sixth century BC) credited as the founder of Greek dramatic tragedy.

29. **Aristophanes:** Greek playwright (c. 450–385 BC) most famous for the comedies *Lysistrata*, *The Birds*, and *The Frogs*.

30. **mistral:** Originating from a word meaning "master wind," a mistral is a strong, cold, northwesterly wind that blows through the Rhône valley and southern France into the Mediterranean Sea.

31. **Triton:** In Greek mythology, a minor sea god generally represented as a man with a fish's tail, carrying a trident and shell trumpet.

32. **Pyramus:** The tragic love story of Pyramus and Thisbe inspired *Romeo and Juliet*. According to Roman mythology, Pyramus was a young man of Babylon who fell in love with Thisbe, a Babylonian maiden. The two were forbidden by their parents to marry and only dared to meet and talk through a chink in a wall. Eventually they conspired to meet secretly outside the city at the tomb of Ninus. Thisbe arrived first, but encountered a lioness who had just made a kill. Frightened by the animal and its bloodied jaws, she fled, dropping her cloak on the ground as she ran. Pyramus arrived shortly afterward and, upon seeing his lover's ripped and bloodstained cloak, became convinced Thisbe had been killed. In his grief, he stabbed himself. Thisbe returned to their meeting place and seeing Pyramus' dead body, took his sword and killed herself.

33. **popinjay:** A vain or conceited person, especially one who dresses or behaves extravagantly.

34. **ballade:** A poem usually composed of three stanzas and an envoi (short conclusion stanza). The last line of the opening stanza becomes the refrain; the same rhymes recur throughout the poem.

35. **Céladon:** The hero in Honoré d'Urfé's pastoral romance *L'Astrée* (1610).

36. **Scaramouche:** In the Italian theatrical *commedia dell'arte* tradition of the sixteenth, seventeenth, and eighteenth centuries, Scaramouche (derived from the Italian for "skirmish") was a stock character who was both a braggart and a coward. Interestingly, years after Rostand's death, author Rafael Sabatini published his novel *Scaramouche: A Romance of the French Revolution* (1921); Sabatini's Scaramouche

was, like Rostand's Cyrano de Bergerac, a complex
hero who was intelligent, witty, and a gifted swordsman.

37. **feint:** A deceptive or pretended blow, thrust, or
other movement in fencing.

38. **D'Artagnan:** Best known from Alexander Dumas'
The Three Musketeers. His cameo appearance in
the play is significant and tongue-in-cheek. D'Artagnan, like Cyrano, was also a seventeenth century
(1623–73) historical figure. Both Dumas' D'Artagnan and Rostand's Cyrano take part in the siege at
Arras.

39. **"Sic transit":** The beginning of a well-known Latin
axiom, *sic transit gloria mundi,* which means "so
passes away the glory of the world." That is, earthly
glory, like Montfleury's fame as an actor, is fleeting.

40. **Silenus:** In Greek mythology, an aged woodland
deity who was responsible for the education of
Dionysus. He is usually depicted as either musical
and dignified, or as an old drunkard.

41. **Cleopatra . . . Caesar:** Prior to forming a romantic
and political alliance with Mark Antony, Cleopatra,
queen of Egypt from 51 to 30 BC, has a brief affair
with Julius Caesar (who became dictator of the
Roman Empire in 48 BC).

42. **Berenice . . . Titus:** Berenice was the great-
granddaughter of Herod the Great of Judea (and
daughter of Herod Agrippa I—the friend of Emperor Claudius). Titus was her lover, but they were
forced to part ways when he became emperor, because he was Christian and she was Jewish. Their
story inspired legions of writers, including Racine.

43. **duenna:** A chaperone and governess.

44. **soubrette:** Minor female role in a comedy, usually a maidservant.

45. **Scipio:** Son-in-law of Scipio Africanus, who defeated Hannibal in 202 BC, concluding the Second Punic War. Publius Cornelius Scipio Nasica Corculum became influential in Roman politics. He led the long opposition against the declaration of the Third Punic War.

46. **Seine:** The river Seine, which flows through Paris to the English Channel, is one of the most famous and scenic Parisian landmarks.

Second Act

1. **Orpheus and the Maenads:** Orpheus, the son of Apollo, was slain by the Maenads, a wild, frenzied group of Dionysians, who happened upon Orpheus wandering in the woods. The Maenads literally tore him to pieces, but Orpheus' still-singing head floated downriver, eventually coming to rest on the shores of the island of Lesbos. From then on, Lesbos became known as the island of poetry.

2. **Phoebus . . . Apollo:** In Greek mythology, Apollo is the god associated with music, poetic inspiration, prophecy, and especially when called by the name Phoebus, with the sun.

3. **Benserade:** Isaac de Benserade, (1613–91), French poet.

4. **Saint-Amant:** Marc Antoine de Gerard sieur de Saint-Amant, (1594–1661), French poet.

5. **Chapelain:** Jean Chapelain (1595–1674), French poet and man of letters.

6. **Marais:** The people of the Marais district.

7. **"Gazette":** The *Gazette* was the first newspaper in France, published weekly, founded by Théophraste Renaudot.

8. **pentacrostic:** An acrostic is a poem in which the first letters of the lines form a word or message related to the subject of the poem. A pentacrostic is a five-part acrostic that repeats the word or message five times.

9. **"Agrippina":** *La Mort d'Agrippine, (Death of Agrippine)*, Cyrano's only tragedy, provoked a scandal when it was performed at the Hôtel de Bourgogne in 1653, thanks to a line that was mistakenly believed to be blasphemous. In 1872, the play was revived for a single performance in Paris.

10. **The chapter of the windmills!:** This refers to chapter 13 of Miguel de Cervantes's novel *Don Quixote* (1605, 1615), in which the character Don Quixote, under the delusion that he is a medieval knight, attacks windmills, mistaking them for monsters.

11. **fusillade:** To attack or shoot down someone by a series of shots fired simultaneously or in quick succession.

12. **letters to Chloris:** In Greek mythology, Chloris is the goddess of flowers and the personification of spring.

Third Act

1. **Capuchins:** Roman Catholic religious order of friars, one of the independent orders of the Franciscans.

2. **Richelieu:** Again, Cardinal Richelieu, minister of France under Louis XIII.

3. **Hercules:** In Greek and Roman mythology, a hero who proved his superhuman strength through the successful completion of twelve seemingly impossible labors.

4. **Diogenes:** A Greek Cynic philosopher who did away with traditional comforts and lived in a tub, he taught that the virtuous life is the simple life.

5. *pater noster:* In Latin, a common name for the Lord's Prayer.

6. **cowl:** A large, loose hood, especially one forming part of a monk's habit.

7. **Lazarus:** According to the Bible, Lazarus was the brother of Mary and Martha who, after four days in the tomb, was brought back to life by Jesus.

8. **balustrade:** A railing on a balcony or terrace.

9. **Algiers:** The capital of Algeria and one of the leading Mediterranean ports of North Africa.

10. **the Great Bear:** The constellation Ursa Major, also known as the Big Dipper. Cyrano refers to traveling through many constellations in the sky.

11. **Trident:** In Greek mythology, a three-pronged weapon borne by Poseidon. It was variously represented as a fishing spear, a goad, or forked lightning.

12. **Sirius:** The Dog Star, the brightest star in the sky, located in the constellation Canis Major.

13. **Regiomontanus:** Regarded as the most important astronomer of the fifteenth century, Regiomontanus was born Johann Müller in Königsberg. He was an early sighter of Halley's comet, constructed an astrolabe, composed writings on calendar reform, wrote four important works on trigonometry and astronomy, and translated Ptolemy's *Mathematical Syntaxis*.

14. **Archytas:** A contemporary of Plato's, this Pythagorean mathematician lived in the fifth century BC.

15. **icosahedron:** A solid figure with twenty plane faces.

16. **Diana:** In Roman mythology, the goddess associated with hunting and virginity.

Fourth Act

1. **the siege of Arras:** France had declared war on Spain in 1635. The siege of Arras was an important step in Richelieu's attempt to conquer Artois. The historical Cyrano was severely wounded at Arras and was forced to retire from military life afterward.

2. **chyle:** Lymph that is milky from emulsified fats.

3. *sallet:* A light fifteenth-century helmet with or without a visor, and with a projection over the neck.

4. **Homer:** Refers to the Greek epic poet of the eighth century BC credited with writing the *Iliad* and the *Odyssey*.

5. **Dordogne:** A river in western France.

6. **Descartes:** René Descartes (1596–1650), the French philosopher and mathematician who concluded that everything is open to doubt except conscious experience.

7. **galantine:** A cold dish consisting of boned meat or fish that has been covered with aspic.

8. **Venus:** In Roman mythology, the goddess of love.

9. **ortolan:** An Old World songbird that was formerly eaten as a delicacy. The male ortolan has an olive green head and yellow throat.

Fifth Act

1. **"How the Devil came he there?":** This famous line from Cyrano's comedy *Le Pédant Joué* is echoed in Molière's *Les Fouberies de Scapin*. Again, Rostand is being somewhat anachronistic and inaccurate: Cyrano's play was published in 1645; Molière's was not performed until 1671, well after Cyrano's death.

INTERPRETIVE NOTES

The Plot

Set in Paris in the year 1640, *Cyrano de Bergerac* is the story of a brilliant and formidable poet and swordsman afflicted with an uncommonly large nose. Deeply in love with his cousin, the lovely and brilliant Roxane, Cyrano believes himself to be too ugly to dare reveal his true feelings for her for fear that she will not return them. Cyrano is a man of great nobility, a loyal protector of his friends (for instance, he protects his friend Lignière from his ambushers, and he prevents Ragueneau from committing suicide). But he has a weak spot: it is said that any man who dares insult Cyrano's nose will soon meet his demise.

From the moment he is introduced, Cyrano demonstrates his wicked wit and temper. Having forbidden the actor Montfleury from performing for a month, Cyrano goes to the Hôtel de Bourgogne only to find that Montfleury plans to act in *La Clorise* that night. Roxane is in the audience, as is a handsome but vapid nobleman, Christian, who tells his friend Lignière that he is in love with Roxane.

A group of aristocrats descends upon Cyrano when he thwarts Montfleury's attempt to take the stage. Cyrano challenges them all to a duel. The Comte de Guiche (Count of Guiche) sends Valvert, the nobleman he has chosen as Roxane's future husband, to intervene. Valvert blandly insults Cyrano's nose, inspiring Cyrano to launch into a lengthy monologue detailing the many ways his nose could have been more imaginatively scorned. When Valvert then insults Cyrano's attire, Cyrano claims that his inner distinctions are more important, and the two duel. As they spar, Cyrano improvises a poem about the duel and, as he utters the poem's last line, dramatically thrusts the sword home. His victory creates a sensation: he is even congratulated by D'Artagnan, the musketeer from Alexander Dumas' *The Three Musketeers*. Cyrano despairs over the impossibility of a union with Roxane, and his friend Le Bret tells him he should tell her how he feels. Then Cyrano receives a message from Roxane's duenna asking him to meet Roxane in the morning; he imagines she must share his undeclared love. Elated, he protects his friend Lignière on the way home.

But when Roxane and Cyrano meet at Ragueneau's pastry shop the next morning, she confides that she loves Christian, who is set to join the Cadets of Gascoyne, Cyrano's company of guards. Secretly dejected, Cyrano agrees to protect Christian. Soon after Roxane's departure, the cadets of the regiment arrive. Christian foolishly tries to prove his courage by arrogantly insulting Cyrano's nose. As the others shudder to see what will become of Christian, Cyrano surprises them all by embracing his insulter; he even tells him about Roxane's feelings. Christian is thrilled but despondent: he knows he is no match for Roxane's intellect. Cyrano proposes a solution: he will write to Roxane, pretending to be Christian.

Cyrano's own romantic sentiments, disguised as Christian's, win Roxane over—but his victory comes at a dear price to Roxane, Christian, and himself. Deception, pride, and unrealistic expectations combine to keep true romantic happiness from blossoming between any of the primary characters of the play.

The Characters

Cyrano de Bergerac. The pen may be mightier than the sword, but Cyrano is equally adept at using both. Cyrano de Bergerac is a member of the Cadets of Gascoyne (a company of guards from southern France) and a talented poet and playwright. His curse, he believes, is his extremely long nose, the one blemish preventing him from attaining true love. Secretly he loves his cousin Roxane, but will never tell her for fear of rejection.

Roxane. Roxane is Cyrano's beautiful, intelligent, and highly desirable cousin. Christian, the Comte de Guiche, and Cyrano (in secret) clamor for her attentions. But Roxane has high expectations, demanding not simply love, but high, romantic love, delivered in witty phrases and soul-baring poetic verse.

Baron Christian de Neuvillette. Christian is an attractive but rather dull-witted young nobleman. Newly arrived in Paris, he falls for Roxane and joins Cyrano's company of cadets. Only with Cyrano's verbal assistance is he able to woo Roxane.

Comte de Guiche. Richelieu's nephew is the villain of the play: a powerful, married nobleman in love with Roxane. A vengeful, manipulative man, he tries to have Cyrano killed on numerous occasions. The Comte de Guiche sends Cyrano and Christian's company of cadets to the war's front lines, presumably to their deaths.

Ragueneau. Ragueneau is one of Cyrano's dearest friends. A pastry chef with a passion for poetry, Ragueneau believes that poetry is quite literally food for the soul. His shop is frequented by poets who come to take advantage of Ragueneau's generous spirit, exchanging poems for sweets. Eventually Ragueneau's wife, Lise, leaves him, his business fails, and he goes to work as a porter for Roxane. He drives Roxane's carriage through enemy lines so she may visit Christian at the war front.

Lise. Ragueneau's critical wife does not approve of her husband's patronage of the local poets. Eventually she leaves him for a musketeer.

Le Bret. Le Bret is Cyrano's close confidant and adviser, a fellow soldier and guardsman.

Lignière. A poet, satirist, and alcoholic, Lignière has managed to acquire a large number of powerful enemies. Although he is a friend of Christian's, it is Cyrano who protects him from the hundred men de Guiche has hired to attack him.

Roxane's duenna. Both companion to and chaperone of Roxane, this governess is supposed, but often neglects, to keep her charge out of danger.

Vicomte de Valvert. The Comte de Guiche tries to arrange a marriage of Roxane to the insolent Valvert, so that de Guiche can conveniently see Roxane as his mistress.

Montfleury. Yet another of Roxane's suitors, Montfleury is an unattractive and untalented actor.

Carbon de Castel-Jaloux. The captain of Cyrano's company of guards is a skilled, successful leader.

Bellerose. He manages the theater at the Hôtel de Bourgogne, where Montfleury takes the stage in the first act of *Cyrano de Bergerac*.

Capuchin. The monk delivers a message from the Comte de Guiche to Roxane. While Cyrano stalls the Comte de Guiche, the Capuchin monk performs Roxane and Christian's wedding ceremony.

Mother Margaret de Jésus, Sister Claire, Sister Martha. These compassionate nuns in Roxane's convent allow Cyrano to make his weekly visits to her.

Symbols and Themes

Cyrano's nose. Cyrano's nose is the most obvious symbol in the play. Although the nose is not actually his Achilles' heel, it symbolizes Cyrano's worst flaw, his utter lack of self-confidence, at least in matters of love. Cyrano sees his huge nose as a blemish on his entire life, an obstacle standing between him and happiness. His nose renders him defensive, quick to pounce on any man who dares stare too closely or, worse, verbally insult him. It skews his vision, at least of himself, so that he is unable to see how a woman as beautiful as Roxane could ever be attracted to him. Cyrano's perception of his nose reveals his inability to realize the importance of inner beauty. Since he cannot see past his own outward appearance, Cyrano never truly appreciates Roxane's inner beauty and her capacity to see his.

Beauty and the Beast, or inner versus outer beauty. As an allegory of inner versus outer beauty, *Cyrano de Bergerac* channels the time-honored tale of "Beauty and the Beast." In this version, Cyrano, symbolizing inner beauty, is in conflict with Christian, who represents outer beauty, for the love of Roxane. Roxane can be said to embody both inner and outer beauty: she is both brains and beauty. Yet at the beginning of the play she is unable to distinguish between the soul and its outward manifestations. This theme is complicated by the fact that Cyrano, although he represents the higher qualities of intellect and integrity, displays them by outward shows of rash temper, flamboyant gesture, swashbuckling dueling, and showy wordplay. So, even when Roxane claims to be able to see past surface beauty and have fallen in love with the "soul" behind the letters, it is arguably actually the outward, verbal display of the letters that she embraces. Inner beauty, and therefore Roxane's love for Cyrano, becomes manifest only at the play's culmination, when she realizes not only the true identity of the letter writer, but the extent of his devotion.

Values and ideals. *Cyrano de Bergerac* places strong emphasis on values and ideals. These qualities are part of what Cyrano calls his "panache." Throughout the play, Cyrano eloquently defends values such as integrity, bravery, glory, patriotism, and loyalty. In fact, Cyrano's adherence to such values prevents him from confessing his love for Roxane and provides the play's major conflict. Even though he and Christian are initially rivals, Cyrano swears to keep his word to Christian, now that they are united by their deception of Roxane and both serve in the same company of guards. As a result of his extreme loyalty, Cyrano protects his secret nearly to his death; his death itself, though tragic, is also transcendent. The ending of the play implies that by keeping to his values and ideals at the cost of his personal desires, Cyrano achieves an ideal, moral, and ultimately heroic status.

Deception. Cyrano's lack of confidence leads to a tangled situation. He offers to help Christian deceive Roxane in hopes that he will eventually win her for himself. But the plan backfires because Cyrano is so successful in his letter-writing, and even, in the balcony scene, at deceiving and wooing Roxane. Ironically his deception leads to what he had tried to avoid all along, the union of Christian and Roxane. Just before Christian's death, when he realizes that Cyrano loves Roxane, and Roxane only loves Christian for Cyrano's letters, Cyrano, with Christian's help, is given the opportunity to "undo" his deception. But Christian's untimely death quickly takes this chance away. To confess the truth to Roxane, that she has fallen in love with a man who never existed, would make a mockery of her mourning and perhaps even turn her against Cyrano. Therefore, in a series of ironies, Cyrano is deceived by his own deceptions and is never able to honestly share his love with Roxane.

Romance and romanticism. Cyrano is often described, and even derided, as a "romantic hero." In fact, Cyrano embraces "romanticism" in the French literary, the French medieval, and the English literary sense of the word. Rostand composed the play only a few decades after the height of the French Romantic movement, a period from about 1827 to 1847. During this time, Victor Hugo was the preeminent French writer, and the plays of William Shakespeare had just been translated into French. With the character of Cyrano, Rostand certainly aspires to Shakespearean heights, and, of course, the balcony scene with Cyrano, Christian, and Roxane parallels that of the doomed lovers in *Romeo and Juliet*. With its sentimental and idealistic treatments of a theme, *Cyrano* also embodies characteristics of the English Romantic period, which went against the preceding tide of restrained neoclassicist thought. Cyrano's independent spirit, his bravado that would defy the attack of a hundred men, are indicative of the wild, free-spirited ideals of the English Romantic era.

A good part of *Cyrano*'s appeal is its ability to present a French hero for all ages. Rostand accomplished this by building on one of the earliest French literary forms, the medieval romance. The chivalric romances of the twelfth and thirteenth centuries championed the idea of courtly love. In fact, actual "courts of love" existed during this period, presided over by noble ladies, who, much like Rostand's Roxane, had high ideals about love and the codes of seduction. The ideals and tradition of courtly love are plainly visible in *Cyrano*—both in Roxane's preferred method of seduction and in Cyrano-as-Christian's expansive meditations on love and romance.

CRITICAL EXCERPTS

Biographical Studies

Crystal R. Chweh, ed. *Readings on Cyrano de Bergerac*. San Diego: Greenhaven Press, 2001.

Not only did Edmond Rostand rely on stories of the "real" Cyrano to create his famous hero, some of Cyrano de Bergerac's most famous exploits were inspired by Rostand's own experiences. As a young boarding student in Paris, Rostand's way with words was legendary:

> Rostand's wife, Rosemonde, offered an anecdote for further motivation for Cyrano de Bergerac. One summer in Luchon, in the Pyrenees, Rostand met a young man who was suffering from unrequited love. The lovesick young man told Rostand that he had done his best, but the woman he loved was indifferent to him. Rostand asked him what he said to the young woman. The man replied,
> "I tell her that I love her."

"And then?"

"I begin all over again."

"And after that?"

"That's all there is."

Rostand offered his help. He began coaching the young man in speech, literary allusions, and style. The coaching worked and the young man won his suit.

Alba della Fazia Amoia. *Edmond Rostand*. Boston: Twayne Publishers, 1978.

This slim volume gives a quick introduction to the life of the author.

The best understanding of Rostand's dramatic ideas, then, is achieved through comprehension of the hero and heroic fervor in the face of life's challenges and vicissitudes. . . . Living their daily lives, Rostand's heroes experience joy and sorrow, they conquer or they pardon, but in each struggle they gain something important: a broader perspective, which adds a new dimension to human existence and renders life nobler and sweeter. . . . The reality of life for Rostand, the poet, is the dream. . . . In *Cyrano de Bergerac,* there is a double dream that corresponds to the double life of Cyrano himself. There is the dream of everyday life, and the dream of personal love. Cyrano's dream is to be extraordinary in everything; his every gesture, every action, is filled with bravura; but Rostand wishes to convey the realization that grace and gentleness can lie hidden in the dream: "panache is often in the sacrifice that we make. . . ." Suffering gives perspective to Cyrano's dream; sorrow enhances his character.

Nicholas Cronk. Introduction to *Cyrano de Bergerac*. Trans. Christopher Fry. New York: Oxford University Press, 1996.

In Cyrano's dying breaths, though all else is doomed, he consoles himself and Roxane with the satisfaction that he never lost his panache. What exactly is panache? Nicholas Cronk explains that, in its primary meaning, panache "refers to the plume of feathers on a helmet, but its figurative sense of 'display, swagger, verve,' is first attested in English in 1898, in the first English translation of *Cyrano*." At the Académie Française reception in his honor, Rostand grandly and explicitly defined panache in his acceptance speech:

> To joke in the face of danger is the supreme politeness, a delicate refusal to cast oneself as a tragic hero; panache is therefore a timid heroism, like the smile with which one excuses one's superiority. Heroes lacking panache are certainly more disinterested than others, since, in making a sacrifice, panache often brings with it an attitude of consolation. A little frivolous perhaps, most certainly a little theatrical, panache is nothing but a grace which is so difficult to retain in the face of death, a grace which demands so much strength that, all the same, it is a grace . . . which I wish for all of us.

Early Reviews and Interpretations

Max Beerbohm. Review of *Cyrano de Bergerac*. *Saturday Review,* July 8, 1898.

Like many critics after him, Beerbohm decides that the merits of the play outweigh its improbabilities. Beerbohm, the *Saturday Review* critic who succeeded

George Bernard Shaw, comes out in favor of romance, calling Cyrano a new kind of dramatic hero.

Realistic figures perish necessarily with the generation in which they were created, and their place is taken by figures typical of the generation which supervenes. But romantic figures belong to no period, and time does not dissolve them. . . . Cyrano will survive because he is practically a new type in drama. I know that the motives of self-sacrifice-in-love and of beauty-adored-by-a-grotesque are as old, and as effective, as the hills, and have been used in literature again and again. I know that self-sacrifice is the motive of most successful plays. But, so far as I know, beauty-adored-by-a-grotesque has never been used with the grotesque as stage hero. At any rate it has never been used so finely and so tenderly as by M. Rostand, whose hideous swashbuckler with the heart of gold and the talent for improvising witty or beautiful verses—Caliban + Tartarin + Sir Galahad + Theodore Hook was the amazing recipe for his concoction—is far too novel, I think, and too convincing, and too attractive, not to be permanent.

Jay B. Hubbell and John O. Beaty. *An Introduction to Drama.* New York: Macmillan Company, 1927.

Although Hubbell and Beaty concur with other critics that *Cyrano de Bergerac* is flawed, they conclude that the play's flaws on paper seem to disappear when performed onstage:

The play has wit, charm, poetry, and theatrical effectiveness; but it lacks consistency of characterization, even in the case of the hero. Each act is very effective in itself, but the five acts do not make a consistent, well-proportioned whole. Nevertheless *Cyrano* is one of the finest of all contemporary plays and is not unworthy of the tradition of Corneille, whose heroic plays it sometimes recalls. . . . On the Elizabethan stage Cyrano might have been the butt of ridicule, but he appeals to the sentiment that lies back of the story of the ugly duckling. Those of us who are not beautiful or handsome are likely to endow ourselves, by way of compensation, with other attractive qualities. On the stage the sharp contrast between extreme ugliness and greatness of soul is startlingly effective. Cyrano, however, is, for all his charm, a bundle of fine points for the actor rather than a living man like [Shakespeare's] Hamlet or Falstaff. And yet on the stage the play is so effective that we are swept off our feet and our critical faculties are paralyzed. Cyrano, if not a great tragedy, is, in spite of its faults, one of the best of contemporary plays.

W. L. Parker. Introduction to *Cyrano de Bergerac.* Trans. Helen Dole. New York: Three Sirens Press, 1931.

According to Parker, *Cyrano de Bergerac* appeals to the fancy rather than the imagination, and its poetry does not measure up to what renowned critic Matthew Arnold termed the "criticism of life."

The play is called a heroic comedy, yet it degenerates almost to opéra bouffe in the fourth act, which also embraces a tragic element in the death of Christian, while the fifth act is filled with sentimental romance—the very last element a true comedy ought to contain. Again, Cyrano is the only character who is a distinct person, and one person with many personages cannot furnish sufficient play of character to equip a great comedy. Comedy there is in certain scenes—as, for example, in the fifth scene of the third act in which Christian fails so egregiously to make the proper sort of love to Roxane, but the suggestion of romantic melodrama is never far removed. In other words, the play seems to be a good deal of a hybrid, to lack the essential unity of a true work of art.

Contemporary Interpretations and Responses

T. S. Eliot. " 'Rhetoric' and Poetic Drama." In *Selected Essays*. New York: Harcourt, Brace & World, 1960.

In his essay " 'Rhetoric' and Poetic Drama," T. S. Eliot sets out to "dissect and reassemble" notions of rhetoric, which he recognizes is often viewed as synonymous with bad writing. Here, Eliot traces the development of rhetoric as a subtle art, which in the work of Shakespeare (and Rostand, to a lesser degree) features what he terms a "progressive variation in feeling." Rhetoric therefore becomes a tool by which writers can convey varying levels of self-awareness in their characters. Specifically, Eliot compares the balcony scenes in *Romeo and Juliet* to the love scenes of Cyrano, Christian, and Roxane in the garden:

Is not Cyrano exactly in this position of contemplating himself as a romantic, a dramatic figure? This dramatic sense on the part of the characters themselves is rare in modern drama. In sentimental drama it appears in a degraded form, when we are evidently intended to accept the character's sentimental interpretation of himself. In plays of realism we often find parts which are never allowed to be consciously dramatic, for fear perhaps of their appearing less real. But in actual life, in many of those situations in actual life which we enjoy consciously and keenly, we are at times aware of ourselves in this way, and these moments are of very great usefulness to dramatic verse. A very small part of acting is that which takes place on the stage! Rostand had—whether he had anything else or not—this dramatic sense, and it is what gives life to Cyrano. It is a sense which is almost a sense of humor (for when anyone is conscious of himself as acting, something like a sense of humor is present). It gives Rostand's characters—Cyrano at least—a gusto which is uncommon on the modern stage. No doubt Rostand's people play up to this too steadily. We recognize that in the love scenes of Cyrano in the garden, for in *Romeo and Juliet*, the profounder dramatist [Shakespeare] shows his lovers melting into unconsciousness of their isolated selves, shows the human soul in the process of forgetting itself. . . .

Cyrano satisfies, as far as scenes like this can satisfy, the requirements of poetic drama. It must take genuine and substantive human emotions, such emotions as observation can confirm, typical emotions, and give them artistic form; the degree of abstraction is a question of the method of each author. In Shakespeare the form is determined in the unity of the whole, as well as single scenes; it is something to attain this unity, as Rostand does, in scenes if not the whole play.

Henry Hewes. Afterword to *Cyrano de Bergerac*. Trans. Lowell Bair. New York: New American Library, 1972.

Which actor has best performed the role of the quintessential French hero? Hewes compares reviews of various Cyranos of stage and screen to examine the actor's role in making Rostand's hero a living entity. The best actors, Hewes finds, are able to show Cyrano as a blend of physical and intellectual impulses. Here is Hewes on the American stage actor Walter Hampden:

The most famous Cyrano in America was that of Walter Hampden, who in four productions between 1923 and 1936 set a world record of playing the role 991 times as compared to Coquelin's 540 times and Richard Mansfield's 380.

Some critics expressed reservations about Hampden's broadsword rather than rapier approach to the role. Percy Hammond in the *New York Tribune* complained for instance that in the duel with Valvert, Hampden "appeared to be more concerned with the fracas itself than with the composition of the famous ballade," so that "you suspected it was not, as he said it was, an improvisation." Nevertheless, the *Tribune* critic ultimately admitted that "despite little rifts, we came away believing we had seen a Cyrano. We had had a friendly realization of a man who had 'loved hatred' and a woman, and who had strived his best to displease. A poet and a cynic, a blustering warrior and a dove, and a lovable adventurer who wished to die 'with steel in his heart and laughter on his lips.'"

Roxanne. Screenplay by Steve Martin. Directed by Fred Schepisi. Performed by Steve Martin and Daryl Hannah. Columbia Pictures, 1987.

Steve Martin wrote and starred in this story of a modern Cyrano, a small-town fire chief extremely sensitive about his improbably large nose. Following is an excerpt from his speech on noses, which parallels Cyrano's in act 1, scene 4, of the Rostand play:

> C.D. All right. . . . Here goes. Let's start with. . . . Obvious. Is that your nose or did a bus park on your face? Meteorological: Everybody take cover. She's going to blow. Sad: Oh, why the long face? Deductive: With an eraser like that, there must be a mighty big pencil around here somewhere. Helpful: If you had some handles for that thing, you'd have a nice set of luggage. Fashionable: You know, it might deemphasize your nose if you wore something larger, like Wyoming. Snide: Table for two? Personal: Well, here we are, just the three of us. Punctual: All right, Delman, your nose was on time, but *you* were fifteen minutes late! . . . Envious: Oh, I wish I were you! To be able to smell your own ear. Naughty: Pardon me, sir, but some of the ladies have asked if you'd mind putting that thing away. . . . Philosophical: You know, it's not the size of the nose that's important, it's what's in it that matters. . . . Humorous: Laugh and the world laughs with you; sneeze and good-bye Seattle.

Daniel Riemer. *National Biases in French and English Drama.* Garland Studies in Comparative Literature. New York: Garland, 1990.

Riemer offers an alternate interpretation of *Cyrano.*

Rather than emerging as a noble hero, Riemer views Rostand's title character as a suffering artist crippled by his fears and ultimately unable to realize his desires:

> For all of his courage, imaginativeness, and bold spirits, Cyrano is both helpless and hapless. For him to assert his independence merely activates hidden, ominous forces already poised to bear down upon and crush him. Flailing about blindly in his rags to defend a scrap of gentility and grace, he strikes us as a ridiculous and lamentable clown. Indeed, the strain and sacrifice that he must endure on behalf of his ideals makes them negative in thrust, self-defeating in aim. . . .
>
> The longing to announce his passion [for Roxane] openly was first daunted by an understandable fear of rejection; thus, to impress her and win her heart he had to conceal his true identity. By using the handsome (but brainless) Christian as his surrogate, he raised a factitious although insurmountable obstacle to the fulfillment of his desires. Though the strategy was clever, he gained only heartache from it and, in a sense, made matters worse for himself by creating a successful rival to his own affections.

QUESTIONS FOR DISCUSSION

People often compensate for shortcomings in one part of their lives (physical appearance, for example) by developing extraordinary skills in other areas. Can you think of anyone you know who, like Cyrano, tries to make the world forget about one of his features by dazzling them with others? Does struggling to compensate for a perceived flaw make these people stronger or better, or would they be happier simply accepting their weaknesses?

Irony abounds in *Cyrano de Bergerac*. It is ironic, for instance, that Cyrano tries to win Roxane by wooing her for Christian, yet is so successful that she indeed falls for Christian. List other instances of dramatic irony in the play.

Why, in your opinion, does Rostand have Roxane marry Christian? What purpose does this serve in the play? How would the play be changed if their marriage did not occur?

Does Rostand prepare the audience for the death of Cyrano and the resolution of his relationship with Roxane? If so, how?

Some critics label Cyrano a noble hero, loyal to the end. Others say he is self-destructive, crippled by his fears, and unable to act on his desires. What do you think? Were his actions admirable or foolish?

Discuss the ways in which each of these characters changes between his first appearance and his last in the play: de Guiche, Roxane, Ragueneau, Christian, Cyrano.

Trace the theme of poetry in the play, from the verse structure in which the play is written, to Cyrano's improvising a ballade as he duels, to Ragueneau's poems-for-pastries trade, to Cyrano's poetic ruminative letters to Roxane. What is the function of poetry in the play? What does it say about the characters? What do you think Rostand is saying about poetry and its power? How do you think Rostand is using poetry to convey larger themes and ideas?

Ultimately, was Cyrano's act of self-sacrifice worth his anguish? Was the love of Roxane worth his suffering?

SUGGESTIONS FOR THE INTERESTED READER

If you enjoyed *Cyrano de Bergerac*, you might also be interested in the following:

To read the writings of the historical Cyrano de Bergerac in English, see Richard Aldington's *Cyrano de Bergerac*, a 1923 translation of Cyrano's *L'Autre Monde, or Voyages to the Moon and the Sun,* published by E.P. Dutton.

Erica Harth's 1970 *"Cyrano de Bergerac" and the Polemics of Modernity,* published by Columbia University Press, offers a critical interpretation of Cyrano's work.

Cyrano on Film

Film versions of the Cyrano de Bergerac story abound. One notable adaptation was director Michael Gordon's 1950 film, *Cyrano de Bergerac,* starring José Ferrer as Cyrano and Mala Powers as Roxane.

More recently, Jean-Paul Rappeneau's *Cyrano de Bergerac* starred Gérard Depardieu in the title role and took the 1990 Academy Awards for Best Foreign Film and Best Costume.

Of course, there's also *Roxanne,* the 1987 popular comedy that puts a fairy-tale ending on Rostand's play. Director Fred Schepisi imagines Cyrano as C. D. Bales, a small-town, large-nosed fire chief played by Steve Martin. Daryl Hannah is Roxanne, a beautiful astronomer and the object of C.D.'s affections.

Cyrano Reimagined in Fiction and Poetry

James Louis Carcioppolo's *The Lost Sonnets of Cyrano de Bergerac* purport to be just that: poems written by Cyrano as he reflects on his life, his loves, as well as his enemies and duels. The illustrated volume was published in 1998 by Lost Sonnet Publishing.

In her 2000 novel, *So I Am Glad* (published by Alfred A. Knopf), contemporary Glaswegian author A. L. Kennedy tells the unforgettable and witty story of a lonely radio announcer whose life is dramatically altered by the arrival of a new boarder—none other than Cyrano de Bergerac himself, back from the dead, with his panache ever intact.

*Introducing the Enriched Classics Books-for-Schools Program**

Get your school involved!

The Enriched Classics Books-for-Schools Program is a great way for teachers, students, and other school representatives to earn **FREE** books for the school library or for classroom use.

How does the Enriched Classics Books-for-Schools Program work?

1. Collect five Enriched Classics proof-of-purchase symbols like the one found at the bottom of this page.
2. Download the Enriched Classics Books-for-Schools official request form from simonsays.com by typing the ISBN for this book (found on the back cover) into the search function and clicking "go." Click on the Enriched Classics book cover that appears. When the next screen appears, click on the link for the official request form. Print out the official request form.
3. Fully complete the official request form.
4. Mail the fully completed official request form plus your five Enriched Classics proof-of-purchase symbols to:
   Enriched Classics Books-for-Schools Program
   Simon & Schuster, 1230 Avenue of the Americas, New York, NY 10020
...and Simon & Schuster will send your school the Enriched Classics book of your choice—**FREE!**

*All Enriched Classics titles published in 2004 feature this special offer.

Get a free copy of an Enriched Classics book when you submit five proof-of-purchase symbols for previously purchased Enriched Classics books and a fully completed Enriched Classics Books-for-Schools official request form. This offer is only open to schools through their representatives (i.e., a student representative or administrator on behalf of the school) or school employees. Please submit all five proof-of-purchase symbols at one time. Please allow 10-12 weeks for delivery. Delivery cannot be guaranteed unless you include your zip code on the official request form. The Books-for-Schools Program is valid in the U.S., Canada (void in Quebec), and Puerto Rico while supplies last. Enriched Classics proof-of-purchase symbols may not be reproduced.

Void where prohibited or otherwise restricted by law. All submissions become the property of Simon & Schuster and will not be returned. Simon & Schuster is not responsible for lost, late, illegible, incomplete, postage-due, or misdirected forms or mail. Requests not complying with all offer requirements will not be honored. Approximate retail value of Enriched Classics book is $3.95.

Offer may not be combined with any other offer.
Offer ends the earlier of April 30, 2005 or while supplies last.

09745

ENRICHED
CLASSICS
Proof of Purchase